Maguire stood up. ～～～～～ man in his late forties, tall and rotund, with his belly sagging over his
belt.

'Washington is extremely worried by the continued
resistance to the siting of Cruise and Pershing in
Britain and Europe . . .

'Our credibility is suffering as the peace movement
makes forward strides. We need action to shout down
the peaceniks.'

'What kind of action?' demanded Capstick.

'. . . What you have to do is plan and organize
yourselves to be on the look out for anything that can
be used against the peaceniks to our advantage. For
example, in the States we're hotting up the war of
words against Libya in order to divert attention from
the nuclear issue. But whatever you choose, the major
criterion of acceptability is that it must originate here,
in Britain. America must not be seen to have a hand
in it.'

Also by James Murphy in Sphere Books:

CEDAR

James Murphy

JUNIPER

SPHERE BOOKS LIMITED

For Jane;
Wife, Mother and inspiration

SPHERE BOOKS LTD

Published by the Penguin Group
27 Wrights Lane, London W8 5TZ, England
Viking Penguin Inc., 40 West 23rd Street, New York, New York 10010, USA
Penguin Books Australia Ltd, Ringwood, Victoria, Australia
Penguin Books Canada Ltd, 2801 John Street, Markham, Ontario, Canada L3R 1B4
Penguin Books (NZ) Ltd, 182–190 Wairau Road, Auckland 10, New Zealand

Penguin Books Ltd, Registered Offices: Harmondsworth, Middlesex, England

First published 1987 by the Malvern Publishing Company Limited
Published by Sphere Books Ltd 1988
3 5 7 9 10 8 6 4 2

Copyright © James Murphy 1987

Made and printed in Great Britain by
Richard Clay Ltd, Bungay, Suffolk
Filmset in Monophoto Ehrhardt

The nuclear arms race has no military purpose. Wars cannot be fought with nuclear weapons. Their existence only adds to our perils because of the illusions they have generated.

Lord Louis Mountbatten: his speech to the Stockholm International Peace Research Institute at Strasbourg, May 11th, 1979, one month before his assassination.

PRELUDE

1979

Copenhagen, Denmark

I

Burton watched the DC-9 touch down from behind the glass of the Observation Gallery. The sun was shining and the electronic notice board told him the outside temperature was well above the seasonal average. Draughts of hot air wafted round his ankles, but he shivered despite the heavy overcoat and thick woollen scarf he wore. He waited until the staircase had been positioned at the front of the aircraft before making his way through to the Arrivals Hall, longing for another cognac.

Dewhurst was one of the last to emerge from customs. He surveyed the waiting faces through his horn-rimmed spectacles rather like a visiting dignitary inspecting a guard of honour. Burton went to meet him and they shook hands limply, said hello, then made for the exit and a taxi which drove them into the city.

Burton paid off the cab outside the Town Hall on the Raadhusplasden, and led the way to the railway station. 'We're going to Bakken.'

'Where?'

'Bakken,' he repeated, as he purchased two tickets for the *S-tog*. 'It's an Amusement Park. Only just opened for the season, so it'll be quiet.'

Dewhurst snorted. 'Amusement Park, eh? Ferris-wheels and merry-go-rounds? Thinks he's a latter-day Harry Lime does he?'

Burton did not say anything. The *S-tog* pulled into the station. He stamped both tickets on the yellow machine as they boarded. 'Bakken is in the central travel area. Yellow stamp. Valid for an hour,' he explained, not because he needed to, more for the sake of something to say. 'The red machine is for outside travel.'

Dewhurst spent the journey staring out of the window, ignoring Burton and his attempts at polite conversation. At Bakken they detrained and Burton paid their entrance into the Park.

'Where'll he be?' asked Dewhurst.

'He said under the Ferris-wheel.'

'I might have guessed,' Dewhurst sneered. He stopped. 'Go and get him. I'm not standing outside with him.' He looked about and pointed. 'Bring him to that café. I could do with some tea.'

II

'It's two hundred and fifty thousand pounds I'll be wanting.' Although Gallagher was looking at Burton, his control, he directed his statement at the short man with horn-rimmed spectacles, who so far had said nothing.

'Look here, Gallagher,' said Burton, clenching his fists. 'We had a deal. Don't fuck with me now.'

Gallagher grinned, and his huge red nose, like a plasticine blob, began to migrate to his cheekbones. 'I will, Mr Burton, I will. Because you tried to take me for a fool.'

'One hundred and twenty-five thousand,' interrupted the little man. 'And the farm in British Columbia. Fully stocked.'

Gallagher continued as if he hadn't heard the new offer.

4

'I've worked with you for over three years. Mr Burton. With your help, my unit have pulled off some of the best jobs for the cause. I'm the most wanted man in Britain. And the I R A have the reputation of callous, murdering swine. You're the good guy chasing me, the bad guy.'

'You've been well paid for it,' snapped Burton. 'A small, bloody fortune.' He finished off his cognac.

'True enough. True enough. And worth every penny of it,' Gallagher said. 'But this proposal.' He sighed. 'I'd be wanted all over the world, never able to show my face again. I'd have to stay buried for ever. The farm'll be my haven, my sanctuary. But I'd need the extra cash to help while away the long, lonely days.'

'One hundred and fifty thousand.' The little man took off his glasses and held them up to the light.

'Thank you,' said Gallagher. 'But this job calls for a quarter of a million. You'll be getting more out of it than you usually do.' Gallagher's eyes, puffed and swollen with drink and full of cunning, darted between the two men. 'The I R A will never recover from this action. They'll be reviled in the West. Recruitment will fall. Donations from America will drop off. And your friends will be jumping all over us.'

'That's what it's all about, Gallagher,' said Burton.

'Is it now? Is it indeed?' He sat back in his seat. 'Is that all that this man's death will mean to your masters?'

'What are you . . .?'

'That'll do, Burton,' interrupted the man. He was polishing his glasses with a pale blue handkerchief. 'Please continue, Mr Gallagher.'

'Thank you,' said Gallagher. 'Now I've been doing a bit of research since you first made this proposal. Not the usual stuff you know. That's all in the history books and biographies. No. What I've been reading is what he's been

5

saying down through the years. Inside and outside the armed forces. What has never been widely reported. Hushed up almost. Until now. You see, there's this Peace Prize he's been awarded. The Louise Weiss Foundation Prize. He'll be collecting it in Strasbourg in May.'

'One hundred and seventy-five thousand.' He put on his spectacles again.

'And we've a fair idea what his acceptance speech will be about. And I bet it'll be widely reported, eh? And certain people, peaceful people, if you take my point, will be very interested. Might even adopt him as their grand old man of wisdom. He could do a lot of harm to your masters. Especially on the nuclear issue. That's what my research tells me.'

'Very good, Mr Gallagher.'

'So there's more to this job than usual. That's why, Mr Burton, I said you tried to make a fool of me. Your side will see a lot more benefits from all this.' He rubbed his hands together. 'It's a quarter of a million, then?'

Burton stood up and went to the counter. He was out of it now. It was between Dewhurst and Gallagher. He ordered another large cognac.

'We'll pay your price,' said Dewhurst. 'It'll be waiting for you in the usual place. After the event. All or nothing on completion.'

Gallagher stroked his chin thoughtfully. 'Okay. Agreed.' He shoved out a big paw, which Dewhurst disregarded. 'And everything will be ready for me in Canada?' he added, leaving his hand occupying the space between them.

'Yes.'

'Then I'll be off.' He got to his feet and inclined his head. 'Be seeing you.' He strode from the cafeteria, his footsteps echoing among the empty booths.

Burton sidled up to Dewhurst's shoulder. 'He'll be heading for Amsterdam. Then Dublin.'

Dewhurst nodded. 'When Mr Gallagher is safely en-sconced on his farm in Canada, say in four or five years' time, when his defences are down, when he thinks the world has forgotten about him, I'm going to send someone over there to cut his throat.' The contempt in his voice was directed at Gallagher. The scorn in his eyes was re-served for Burton.

London, England

I

Maitland and Craig were giggling to themselves. They weren't drunk though they had been drinking most of the day; but they had the giggles, the alcohol they had consumed prompting them to exaggeration. The object of their augmented mirth was the elderly lady in front of them at the carousel, who turned from time to time to scowl at the pair of inebriates. The other passengers from the Paris flight waiting to collect their luggage tried to ignore the trio in the way most English travellers tend to do when faced with the untoward, by developing acute symptoms of myopia and deafness, coupled with an urge to keep the head moving.

'We'll have one in the lounge bar, then we'll go back to my place,' suggested Craig.

'Sorry, old boy,' said Maitland. 'I'm two days overdue already. They'll have my balls if they find out about this.'

'Or rather she will,' said Craig, indicating the woman in front and breaking into a bout of suppressed laughter. He put his arm around Maitland's shoulder to steady himself.

The elderly lady turned and glared balefully at them. Maitland tried hard not to laugh. He could still see her in the Departure Lounge at Charles De Gaulle, clinging passionately to the hipless young beau who had showered her with kisses prior to boarding the flight. 'Rich mutton dressed as mutton,' had been Craig's comment, and that had started the hilarity and the jokes that had entertained them on the short haul to London.

'Oh God,' said Craig, wiping the tears from his eyes. 'I haven't laughed so much since mother disinherited brother Peter.'

'Come here,' whispered Maitland urgently. He pulled Craig in front of him and ducked his head.

'What?' said Craig.

'Keep still.' There was no humour in the voice. 'I've just seen Burton. My boss.'

'Where?' Craig tried to turn round to look.

'Keep still! Don't look now. He's over there, at the next carousel.'

'Has he spotted you?'

Maitland peered round Craig's bulk. 'I don't think so. Otherwise he'd have been over here creating.'

'What are you going to do?'

'Get out of here as fast as I can and get the next flight to Belfast.'

'But what if he's going back there? On the same flight?'

'I don't think so. He's with somebody. He's just handed him his case.'

'Anyone you know?'

'Yes. Dewhurst.'

Craig's eyes opened wide. '*The Butcher?*'

'The very same.' Maitland adjusted his position. 'They're going.' He watched them as they followed the green line through customs.

'Here come the bags,' said Craig, pulling himself free. Both men were now sober.

Maitland pushed forward to find his weekend bag. 'I wonder what those two were doing together?' he said over his shoulder to Craig. 'On a flight from . . .' He glanced at the board above the carousel. '. . . Copenhagen?'

9

II

'It is too late for second thoughts,' said Dewhurst. 'The role of Henry the Second does not become you.'

'While that of William de Traci dispensing with the troublesome cleric fits you like a glove,' retorted Sir Robert MacKenzie. He stood with his back to the door.

'I make no apologies. I am simply doing my duty.'

'Duty?' cried MacKenzie. He bowed his head. 'If this ever gets out . . .'

'If it does, there will be a holy row. We will be exiled, as it were. Just like Becket's killers,' said Dewhurst. 'And when they see the necessity of our act, will we be given the glory?'

'Is that what you want?'

'Our task is to defend this nation irrespective of who is in power: not only to guard the democratic institutions against external, hostile elements, but also internally, to protect those same institutions against the consequences of democracy itself.' Dewhurst paused for a moment. 'You've heard that before now, haven't you? It was you who told me that too much freedom was just as dangerous as too little. Remember?' MacKenzie did not answer. Dewhurst continued. 'You were Operations Chief, then. You used that argument, those fine words, to persuade me to join your select group that was intent on destabilizing Wilson's Socialist government in the early seventies.'

MacKenzie glowered at Dewhurst who was again rattling MacKenzie's skeleton in the cupboard to ensure his full cooperation and agreement. 'I have to go, Alan,' he said, stiffly. He retreated from the room without another word.

No sooner had he gone, than Nike marched in, brisk and business-like. 'Nike, I want you to keep an eye on our friend Burton. The strain is becoming too much for him. He drinks.' Nike bared his teeth. Dewhurst smiled. 'And he is beginning to cause problems.'

Newry, Northern Ireland

I

Maitland showed his passes to the armed RUC officer at the entrance to Newry Police Barracks, then went inside where he had to repeat the process at the desk. One or two of the officers in the lobby exchanged greetings with him. Robbie Woods met him as he climbed the stairs to his room on the second floor.

'Back, are we?' asked Woods with a grin.

'Just,' replied Maitland. He was still hungover and the early morning drive up from Belfast, where he had spent the night, had not helped.

'I'll brew some tea,' said Woods, and went downstairs.

Maitland collapsed in his chair, buried his head in his hands, and Woods found him in that position when he returned with a mug of tea.

'I've put a raw egg in it. My ma's recipe.'

'You must be kidding,' replied Maitland, taking the tea. He sipped it cautiously. 'Has Mr Burton tried to contact me?' he added casually, between sips.

Woods shook his head. 'No. You're fine. Nobody missed you.'

'Any other messages, then?'

'Willie Galton wants to see you. Rather urgently. He was in first thing but then had to go out. He said if you were back, you were to meet him at half eleven at the bridge.'

'Okay.' Maitland leaned back in his seat and put his feet on the desk. Woods took the hint and silently withdrew. 'Eleven-thirty,' Maitland reminded himself as he closed his eyes and set his mental alarm clock.

He felt guilty. He should have spent the long weekend at home with his mother instead of living it up with Craig in Paris. What made it worse was that he would have used his mother's illness as an excuse for his absence if Burton had discovered he had been out of the country. He had been lucky; a rare occurrence, a quiet weekend in Northern Ireland, and Burton away as well, with Dewhurst in Copenhagen. He wondered if Burton's trip had anything to do with his poor showing of late. Maitland and his fellow officers liked Burton, but he was drinking too much, especially in the office. It was noticed, and his work was suffering. They tried to help out whenever they could, but Burton was an obstinate old sod, and would persist with a course of action even when it was shown to be incorrect or foolhardy. Drink was the cause of that, thought Maitland. Burton's judgement was becoming increasingly suspect. And Dewhurst's presence demonstrated that London were aware of the problem.

Maitland had the notion to beard Burton in his office, to tell him to go away on holiday, to forget the work, to relax and enjoy himself, as he did on his mad thrashes with Craig. It was the only way to keep one's sanity in the boilerhouse atmosphere of Northern Ireland.

II

Galton saw Maitland coming towards the bridge. He began to move off when he was sure Maitland had seen him. He had not gone more than a few paces, when the heavens opened. Slanting sheets of rain poured from the sky sending the few pedestrians scattering for shelter. Galton waited for Maitland to catch up, and then they set off at a trot looking for a likely place to wait out the sudden storm.

'In here Willie,' Maitland shouted, opening the door into O'Connell's bar. Galton followed.

The floor was wooden, as was the bar, though the latter had seen most of the wear and tear. There were three or four rough tables standing in front of a dirty red bench seat that ran around the wall, but no stools; they were too handy as weapons. Dan O'Connell sat behind the bar trying to polish the name of a well-known lager from the glass he was holding.

'I'll have to be telling you, gentlemen, that we don't start serving until midday,' said Dan, without looking up. 'It's only a quarter to twelve.'

Galton, still holding the door open, paused, and then turned to go. Maitland held on to his elbow. 'Do you mind if we wait in here out of the rain?' He pointed to his coat which was dripping wet.

'Not at all. Not at all. Take a seat.' Dan continued his polishing.

Galton and Maitland took the table nearest the bar. 'How was your holiday, Ollie?' asked Galton as they sat down.

'Fine. Or at least I think it was,' he laughed. 'I don't remember a great deal.'

'Excuse me now,' interrupted O'Connell. 'Would either of you gentlemen like a drink while you're waiting for opening time?' Maitland glanced at Galton who shrugged and smiled. They ordered two pints of porter.

After swopping stories for a few minutes, Galton hinted at the reason for the summons. 'Jimmy-Jack says he needs a holiday. A long one.' They left the bar when the first legitimate customer of the day entered.

III

Galton swung the car round the tight bend and past the school, framed by the purple-black of Slieve Gullion silhouetted against the dark sky. The sudden manoeuvre awakened Maitland who sat up with a start and grunted his surprise. He smacked his dry lips together and glanced across at Galton who was now braking as they approached the chicane leading to the bridge across the gurgling river. The rain had stopped.

The village was quiet and deserted; they passed the church and ascended the hill towards the Priest's mountain. On their right the square, sullen shapes of a new housing development made an angular contrast to the smooth, mushroom contours of the lively oaks and beeches scattered throughout the undulating pastureland. Galton changed down a gear as the car lost impetus on the climb, and he nimbly double declutched into second as he followed the curve of the road left, only to swing sharply right and enter a narrow lane which rose steeply through a tunnel of branches. He began to slow down.

Maitland reached over into the back seat and armed himself with the Ingram machine-pistol; Galton had his already, cradled on his lap. Galton stopped the car and turned off the lights. Both men checked their weapons, then sat in silence, waiting, the cooling tick of the engine counting off the seconds. The digital dashboard clock showed twenty-three fifty-two.

Maitland rolled down his window and poked his head outside, but he could see nothing in the inky darkness, not even the road ahead to Forkhill, nor the side turning which meandered up to the priest's house. *Bandit country*.

He was startled by a sudden click as Galton opened his door and stepped into the road. Maitland followed and felt his feet sink into the mud at the side of the road. He caught his coat in a stream of brambles and he cursed softly to himself as he struggled to extricate himself from the squelching ooze and the stubborn foliage. He joined Galton at the front of the car sucking a bleeding finger, as the moon broke through the barricade of clouds. The wind had dropped and the tinkle of a small brook could be heard above the rustle of branches. Galton led the way forward to the iron gate set in the crumbling wall which they both climbed, dropping down into the long grass that bordered the gravel path. They crept forward, guns at the ready.

The cottage was low, long and uncared for. Its white-washed façade was peeling and cracked, and part of the roof had collapsed and brought down a gable end. The front door had been smashed in, and a feeble attempt at repair had left it looking like a hastily constructed orange box. The windows, all without glass, were shrouded and blank, the hooded eyes of a weary, dying animal.

Galton pushed the door with his toecap: it creaked open, and he went inside. The sound of leather-soled shoes sliding across stone greeted Maitland as he entered. A match flared. 'The door,' hissed a voice. Maitland knocked it closed with his heel.

The pinpoint of light wavered then moved upwards. A chain clinked, and the light burst into a crescent of glowing yellowness as the mantle caught. Jimmy-Jack made the final adjustments then returned to the only chair in the room. Galton was in the other room, checking it out.

'Ah. Mr Oliver. Glad you could make it,' said Jimmy-Jack. Galton came in and stood next to Maitland.

'What's it all about, Jimmy-Jack?' asked Maitland. His attitude to the Irishman was ambiguous and contradictory. On the one hand, he was grateful for the information and help that Jimmy-Jack supplied: it saved lives. On the other, though, he was repelled by the man, who was, after all, a traitor to his own kind. He therefore kept his dealing with Jimmy-Jack on a purely neutral, business level, and never allowed his own feelings to surface.

'It's as I was telling your man there,' said Jimmy-Jack, scratching his left ear. 'I think they're on to me.' Jimmy-Jack's ears were too small for his head, and, as if they were aware of the fact, had, since birth, made ready for flight, jutting out from the sides like the handles of a loving-cup.

'But you don't know for sure?' asked Maitland.

'The only way I'll know for certain is when they put a black bag over my head and blow me away.' He stood up. 'And I'm not waiting around for that to happen. Besides, if they didn't suspect me before, they will now.'

Maitland glanced at Galton. 'He used the Crossmaglen unit to get over the border to here. Said he was going down to Newry as part of the back-up on the attack on the Barracks next week.'

'So. You've burnt your boats, Jimmy-Jack? A foolish thing to do without my say so,' said Maitland angrily.

'But I've not come empty-handed. I've brought over enough with me to pay for my pension in Canada.'

Mullaghmore, Irish Republic

Nike was using a pair of rubber-armoured Zeiss *Dialytes*. He watched the Great Black standing on the sandy shore surrounded by a flock of squawking Common Gulls. Burton shifted and jarred his elbow.

'Sit still.'

'Fuck off,' complained Burton petulantly. 'I'm cold. And I've got cramp.'

Nike glanced at him with contempt. 'Sit still,' he repeated menacingly. Burton took a swig of brandy from his hip flask and curled up in a ball on his side, pulling the sleeping bag up over his head. 'Fucking office boy,' swore Nike. He raised his binoculars again and scoured the beach.

A child in wet bathing trunks that sagged at the bottom to the back of its knees tottered down to the water's edge carrying a bucket with no handle. A woman, hair in curlers, with a body as white as lard barely contained by a twisted black bikini, waved at the child, while another clung to her knees. A man lay nearby on a towel, a handkerchief covering his face, hands clasped on a hairy paunch, his legs two sticks of polished ivory.

Nike moved the glasses on to the harbour wall, followed it out to sea, then brought the glasses to bear on the boats lying at anchor. He picked out *Shadow V* easily enough, a twenty-nine footer, moored at the private jetty. There was no one on board.

He changed position, accidentally kicking Burton in the

18

small of the back. Burton groaned. Nike smiled. He re-focused the binoculars to take in the Victorian gothic mansion, built by Lord Palmerston, that dominated the headland. It was known locally as Classiebawn Castle. There was activity there. A police car was driving up to the main gates and several of the house's occupants were outside on the lawn. He checked his watch. They were later than usual for their lobster hunt. But the old man was ready to go. Dressed in a T-shirt, shorts, and a battered sailor's hat, he seemed to be urging the others to hurry up.

'What's going on?' asked Burton.

Nike could smell the brandy on his breath. 'Getting ready to leave, I think.'

'Thank God for that.'

It was Dewhurst who had insisted that Burton came along. Nike would have preferred to be alone. He didn't like baby sitting drunks, particularly those like Burton who had no regard for roughing it. The man had bitched and complained all night about the cold and the damp, and had kept him awake until the early hours. Nike reckoned that Burton was lucky still to be alive.

Their hide was on the headland, under a rocky outcrop, well hidden by the bounteous spread of gorse, heather and fern. Nike had chosen the site the previous week after a brief reconnoitre; security in the area, as promised, was negligible and he had had no problems or interference.

He aimed the binoculars at the twisting road that led from the house down to the harbour which lay at the tip of a rocky peninsula jutting out into Donegal Bay. He could make out several small fishing smacks at sea and he examined them individually as they basked in the twinkling sunlight and wondered which one Noxy Gallagher was using.

An hour passed before the entourage set off from the house. The police car followed the Land Rover right up to the jetty and the two officers watched and waited until the holiday makers were all safely aboard *Shadow V*, and the old man had taken the helm. Nike's eyes were strained. He put down his glasses and nudged Burton. 'Here. Have a look.'

'No thanks,' said Burton, and curled up in his sleeping bag.

'Suit yourself.' Nike rubbed his eyes fiercely, waited for them to clear, then resumed his watch. The boat was moving forward. He heard the engines roaring as the vessel cleared the harbour wall. He spotted the first of the lobster pot floats bobbing on the water, and listened to the changing pitch of the engine as the old man went full astern for a few seconds and then cut the engine.

There was silence. The vessel drifted towards the floats, the bluish waves lapping against the bows, a gentle reminder of the awesome power below. Nike had the man fixed in his sight. He saw him half turn and mouth some words, gesticulating with his right hand while the left rested on the wheel. Nike braced himself.

The boards suddenly erupted beneath the old man's feet, and he shuddered and shook momentarily, caught in a pulsating capsule of air before disappearing in a flash from Nike's view.

Shadow V came apart at the seams as it was engulfed in a raging blossom of red and orange. The ferocious thunder of the explosion reached the hide seconds later and brought Burton scrambling to his knees to witness the carnage.

Nike's glasses were now filled with a scene from hell: a blazing inferno wallowed on the churning sea, spouting lumps of wood and steel, and discharging great black plumes of smoke that hung accusingly in the clear, sunny sky.

The old man was undoubtedly dead, thought Nike. The bomb had been directly below his feet when Gallagher had detonated it.

Belfast, Northern Ireland

Maitland had been only nine years old when President Kennedy had been murdered. His mother had woken him on the Saturday morning to tell him of the assassination, and, even today, he could remember that particular moment above all others from his childhood. Other people, older than himself, could also recall with amazing clarity what they were doing and saying when they first heard the tragic news from Dallas. It was as if time was quiescent, as if the world could not digest the fact that a man who had been brought smiling into so many homes by the wonder of satellite television, had been seen to be brutally slain through the same medium.

Mountbatten's death struck Maitland in much the same way. He had been driving up from Lisburn when the radio announcer had blurted out the few bare facts available. Maitland had been stunned. He had reached for the volume knob and his hand had seemed to travel in slow motion. By the time he had reached the Holding Centre in Castlereagh, the murder had been confirmed. Grim, angry faces had greeted him. Hardly anybody spoke, and, when they did, it was in grunts through tight lips. Noxy Gallagher was all that was needed to be said.

Later, alone in his office, Maitland's thoughts of Kennedy reminded him of America and the question he would always ask himself when confronted with bloody murders; why, in a country where the word communism was a swear word, did wealthy Americans place millions of dollars into the coffers of the IRA for the purchase of Libyan arms for the fight to establish a Marxist republic in a unified Ireland? He had never been able to discover the answer, and did not think he ever would. Meanwhile, Mountbatten of Burma was yet another victim of the terrorists, as were the eighteen soldiers blown to pieces at Warrenpoint, news of which had just been received.

He spent most of the day checking through Gallagher's file, searching for something, anything, that might have been overlooked and which could possibly betray a chink in the man's armour which, so far, had enabled him to elude the clutches of all the security services in Britain for over three years. But there was nothing. Just a brief case history and voluminous reports of alleged sightings, the most recent being from Copenhagen and Amsterdam on the same day back in April. The man appeared to move easily across frontiers with impunity. Nothing had ever come of any of the sightings. Maitland doubted whether anything would.

It would be six years before Maitland would have cause to recall that sad day in Northern Ireland: six years before he could give some substance to two of the sightings recorded in Gallagher's dossier.

Kabul, Afghanistan

There was a sudden burst of gunfire. Hasham rolled instinctively out of his bunk and lay on the stone floor listening. In the corridor, he could make out the slap of running feet and the high-pitched babble of terror, interspersed with the chatter of automatic weapons. A coup? Another shoot-out between Presidential aides? Something stirred in the room. He could make out the huddled forms of the other servants trying to bury themselves deeper into their blankets. He found his knife and crawled on all fours to the door. He prised it open slowly.

A figure flashed by. Then another. He jumped up and grabbed the third one by the scruff of the neck.

'The Russians. The Russians,' shrieked the man. His breath was foetid, as if the panic and fright had curdled it. He struggled against Hasham's grip. 'They are killing everybody. Let me go, for the love of Allah, let me go!' Hasham released him, and he fled along the gloomy passageway.

The staccato beat of the gunfire was closing in. Hasham ran to the corner, peered round into the murkiness of the kitchen, then leapt up the back stairs to the Presidential quarters.

As he neared the top, he heard the bolt on the iron door being pulled. He pressed his body flat against the roughcast wall. Metal tapped on metal. In the dim light, he saw the barrel of a Kalashnikov assault rifle probing through the opening. He held his knife in his right hand.

24

A Russian soldier emerged. Hasham drove the knife upwards into his throat and gave it a vicious twist. The soldier's knees buckled. Hasham swung round, the knife still in place, and allowed the body to collapse into his arms. He lowered it to the floor. He cocked an ear. The shooting was sporadic now, seeming to come from the vicinity of the dining rooms and kitchen. He took the rifle and an extra magazine from the corpse, and crept forward.

The Afghan guards in the ante-room had been caught unawares. A naked woman lay atop one of the men in the centre of the room, the pair locked together in a bloody embrace. The other four men had died where they sat, in a line facing their friend's exhibition. Blood covered the floor, the walls and part of the ceiling. The smell of cordite, the stench of evacuated bowels, clung oppressively to the air.

In the next room, two more dead men, one still clutching a hand of cards. A young girl, like a bundle of discarded clothes, was sprawled obscenely across an upholstered chair, her head almost severed from her body. The blazing lights enabled Hasham to pick out every detail in one careful glance. He moved on, the Kalashnikov leading the way.

President Hafizullah Amin of Afghanistan lay on his back in the enormous four-poster bed. He was naked. He had been shot at close range in the chest and his throat had been cut. His two female companions, young French blondes, were stretched out at his feet. Both had been shot in the face. Their hair, awash with blood, was plastered to the sheets, and a knife protruded from each vagina.

Footsteps. In the background, the tempo of the gunfire had increased. Hasham tiptoed to the door. It began to open.

Hasham watched from behind the door as Colonel Baye-renov of the KGB went up to the foot of the bed to examine the handiwork of his commandos. He prodded the body of the late President with the muzzle of his Maka-rov pistol.

'Keep your pistol where it is, Bayerenov,' said Hasham.

The Colonel looked up quickly, and located Hasham's shadowy form as it emerged into the light. 'Talebov!' he said, surprised. 'Is that you?' He took a step forward. 'You even look like one of them.' He laughed.

'Stay where you are,' commanded Talebov. He raised the assault rifle. Bayerenov stood still.

'Who gave the order for this?' He indicated the bodies. 'This slaughter.'

'They had grown impatient of you, Colonel,' said Bayerenov. 'Two months to kill one man? Hardly what you would call efficient,' he sneered.

'Amin was to die quietly. On his own. It was to look as if members of his own entourage had murdered him. Why do you think I was sent in the first place? Just to get in some practice as a kitchen porter?'

'You failed, Colonel Talebov. I was ordered to make amends for the GRU's lapse.'

'Like this?' He spat out the words in anger.

'There are to be no survivors. No witnesses. It was neces-sary.'

'The whole country, the whole world, will know about it in a day or two. They will blame us, with or without wit-nesses.'

'I have my orders,' said Bayerenov.

'And what about me? Am I to be included in your clean-ing up operation?' Talebov had tried three times to kill Amin by poisoning the fruit juices he drank so frequently. But the old devil was too cagey. He always made his bodyguards test them first, mixing together several juices from different sources. One or two of his attendants had ended up with stomach upsets, but nothing more serious than that. And now Bayerenov had conducted this bloody massacre on the orders of some impatient idiot in the Kremlin.

'I will bring you out, now that I have found you,' said Bayerenov.

'If I hadn't found you, I would have died like them, I take it?'

Bayerenov shrugged. He holstered his Makarov. 'Stay close to me. Let's go.'

They left the bedroom and headed towards the main staircase. The shooting continued, but now there was a new note. The inmates of the Palace were fighting back. Small arms crackled out replies to the rattle of the Kalashnikovs.

As they came downstairs, they could see the results of the massacre spread before them. Bodies were strewn on the marble floor of the open expanse of the Great Hall. The huge crystal chandelier, suspended from the ornately carved ceiling, had been shattered by a burst of gunfire, and visibility was poor in the dull light which was masked by layers of gunsmoke.

At the bottom of the stairs, the two men stood shoulder to shoulder. The fighting appeared to be confined to the outside of the Palace. 'This way,' said Talebov. He led the way towards the library.

Suddenly Colonel Bayerenov exploded into a multi-coloured ball of blood and guts. He was thrown backwards by the force of the impact and landed in a heap beneath a portrait of President Amin. Colonel Talebov returned the fire, aiming for the darkened recess which was spewing forth a scything hail of bullets. A second weapon opened up from the same direction. Talebov dropped to his knees, firing as he did so, but not before he felt the shudder of bullets tearing open flesh, and the warm wash of his own blood coursing down his rib cage. As his ammunition came to an end, his eyes drooped and he fell forward on to his face, hearing nothing more, his mind delighting him with memories of sunny days and clear mountain air.

EPISODE

1983–84

London, England

I

Maitland left the dance floor. The heat was too much for him, his trousers were sticking to his thighs, and he could feel dampness in his armpits.

'Can't take the pace?' shouted Jack Craig in his ear, as he led his nubile fiancée on to the floor.

Maitland slapped him on the back. His reply was swallowed by the riffs of Eric Clapton's guitar work as *Layla* blasted forth from the disc-jockey's speakers.

Crossing the hallway to the dining room, where the bar was installed, Maitland untied his bow tie, pulled it off and put it in his pocket. He was not looking where he was going. As he reached for the doorknob, he collided with a young woman. She bounced off him and fell against the wall.

'I do beg your pardon,' apologised Maitland. He put out a hand to steady her, and gripped her bare shoulder. 'Are you okay?'

She blinked several times then smiled. 'No stars,' she said, and removed Maitland's hand. 'It was my fault really. I was in such a hurry, I wasn't looking where I was going.' She sounded breathless.

The door opened and Maitland stepped aside to allow a couple to leave. 'I was just going for a drink. Can I get you one?'

'So was I. Yes,' she said, and they went to the bar.

'What would you like?'

'Champagne, please.' Her green eyes sparkled. She walked away.

Maitland ordered the drinks and carried them over to the chiffonier where his new-found companion was awaiting him.

'I'm Oliver Maitland, by the way,' he said, and gave her the glass.

'I know.' She sipped her champagne. 'I'm Julia Parry.'

'Ah!' said Maitland. 'Jack Craig mentioned your name earlier. Rita's cousin.' He peered into her décolletage.

'We have met before you know. At Jack and Rita's engagement party.'

'Sorry. I can't recall,' said Maitland apologetically. 'I wasn't . . .'

'That's twice you've said sorry to me. And we've only been together five minutes. It doesn't augur well for the future,' said Julia, blinking flirtatiously.

Maitland laughed. 'Immediate or long term?' She was stunning in her cream off-the-shoulder dress which accentuated her long auburn hair. Maitland felt a flush of excitement.

'That depends,' said Julia and moved closer to him. 'We also met last year, at this very same New Year's Eve party. You have a habit of ignoring me.' She stepped back. 'But you were very drunk at the time so I suppose you have an excuse.'

'That's just an impression I give when I'm enjoying myself.'

'Which probably accounts for your appalling memory and the tendency to be overly apologetic. You don't know what you've been missing.'

Before he could reply, Julia shoved her glass at him. 'Can I have a refill, please?'

II

Julia prodded the cuttlefish segment. 'What is it?' They were standing in the hall of Maitland's apartment.

'It's a parakeet. An Indian ring-neck. Male gender, named Gussie.'

'Beautiful pink colour on the neck,' said Julia. She ran a finger across the bars. 'Is it yours?'

'No, I'm looking after it for a chap at the office. He's been posted overseas temporarily.' The bird had begun squawking as soon as he had opened the door, and the din had made Julia jump.

'Can he talk?'

'Well, he studied languages at Oxford,' replied Maitland.

'The parakeet I mean, silly,' said Julia. He helped her out of her coat and directed her through into the living room.

'He does, but only with a Scottish accent. I can't understand him.' Maitland left her and went into the bedroom where he hurriedly began to tidy the mess, straightening the duvet and the pillows, bundling together some dirty shirts, and kicking odd socks and balls of fluff under the bed.

She was rifling through his record collection when he rejoined her. 'Help yourself. Classical on the right, modern on the left,' he said. She was very direct, very self-confident, he thought. But not pushy. It had been her suggestion that they leave the party before midnight.

'I can't bear the slushy sentimentality of Auld Lang Syne,' she had said. 'Let's go back to your place.'

So they had. The New Year had been welcomed in on

the taxi journey to Maida Vale. He had kissed her, and she hadn't objected. Maitland's impression was that if he hadn't made the first move, then she would have done.

'We'll have some Brahms,' she said. 'How does this thing work?' She frowned at the compact mini-stack.

Maitland came to her rescue. She sat down on the sofa, gazing up at the Michael Carlo print. 'I like it,' she said finally.

'Thanks,' said Maitland. 'How about a drink?'

She shook her head. 'A coffee, if you don't mind. I have to be on duty at seven.'

Julia was a physiotherapist at the Princess Alexander Hospital. He supposed that her confidence with men sprang from her daily contacts with them on the wards, and the fact that they relied upon her for help. That, and her good looks.

Maitland went into the kitchen and began to percolate the coffee. He drank a glass of milk to settle his stomach which had become upset on the drive home. He placed two mugs on the worktop and found some fairly fresh cream in the refrigerator.

'Do you take sugar?' he shouted above the sound of the *Violin Concerto in D-major*. There was no reply.

He went back to the living room. She had turned off all the lights except for the standard lamp in the corner, and switched on the electric fire, the heat from which caused the streams of Christmas cards around the fireplace to move gently in the draught. He caught the scent of his mother's favourite perfume, *Calèche*, by Hermès. Julia had taken off her shoes, and was curled up on the sofa, her legs folded close to her body, a cushion beneath her head.

She was fast asleep.

III

The growth and strength of the peace campaign in Britain, Europe and the United States is the most impressive phenomenon of this decade. It is impressive because it is so widely spontaneous. And like other spontaneous popular movements of the past, it lacks leadership and central control. However, it has already achieved such dimensions that we ignore it at our peril. Thus it has to be stopped in its tracks before it becomes centralised, and leaders emerge.

It is self-defeating to try and counter the peace campaign by labelling it as a communist-inspired movement. True, communist agents and agitators have tried, and will continue, to exploit the movement. But these are routine political tactics similar to those we employ in directing the anti-peace campaign lobby. Communist input into the movement is insignificant.

It is also counter-productive to portray the campaign as some sort of neutralist movement with an inbuilt desire to lie down and accept Soviet hegemony as a way of evading the responsibilities of national defence. We have to recognize the fact that many of the peaceniks accept the need for national defence, but simply do not believe that nuclear weapons are an acceptable answer.

No. At the core of the movement against nuclear weapons lies a very basic and powerful motivation. The will to survive. To survive as individuals, as families, as members of civilisation. And it manifests itself in a real and vociferous exasperation aimed at the politicians. We are not confronted by dissidents, subversives or revolutionaries. We are fighting the survival instinct. And that is quite senseless.

The instinct to survive is the most potent. Once alerted,

35

aware of a threat, once an enemy is perceived, it
...ie down until that threat is removed. Permanently.
...emy must be destroyed before the instinct subsides.

...ie great success of the peace movement is that they have made the issue of nuclear weapons a simple choice between life and death. The campaign has awakened and aroused the survival instinct in millions of our citizens; a raw nerve has been exposed. The peaceniks have pointed a finger at the bomb, the enemy, and shown it to be a dire threat to mankind. And as the peace campaign gathers momentum, the survival instinct will be rekindled in more and more of our people.

We cannot fight the peaceniks through political and judicial pressures since we are combatting an inherent impulse that will not subside until the threat of the bomb is removed.

The only way in which we can make progress against the peace campaign is by diverting the focal point. At the moment, the bomb is the centre of attention. That is the perceived enemy. In its place we must substitute another enemy, equally as diabolical and destructive, just as tangible and real, equivalently dangerous and threatening. But an enemy we control, one we can manipulate and direct, one through which we can channel the survival instincts of the objectors.

'Some of you may have recognised the star of our little movie,' said Maguire, as the lights came on. 'Professor Irving Bernhardt. Back home, in the States, he is a well-known Industrial Psychologist. He is consultant to some of our major corporations. And when he is not doing that, he is a Chief Adviser on Psychological Warfare Techniques at the National Security Agency. I believe you have met him once or twice, haven't you, Jim?'

'Yes. Several times in fact,' Jimmy Capstick confirmed.

'Right,' said Maguire. 'The point the Professor was making is one that has been made before in a variety of ways. But it is a point on which we all agree. Am I right?'

The head of the CIA's London Station glanced around the room for confirmation.

Sir Robert MacKenzie, Director-General of MI5 said yes, as did Jimmy Capstick, Chief of MI5's Counter-subversive Branch. Alan Dewhurst, in charge of Operations for MI5, simply nodded his head.

Maguire stood up. He was a big man in his late forties, tall and rotund, with his belly sagging over his belt. 'Washington is extremely worried by the continued resistance to the siting of Cruise and Pershing in Britain and Europe.' He crossed his thick arms behind his back. 'Our credibility is suffering as the peace movement makes forward strides. We need action to shut down the peaceniks.'

'What kind of action?' demanded Capstick.

'We need to apply the Professor's theories in the form of some scheme or plan, a series of plans really, that will divert attention from nuclear weapons, and cut the ground from beneath the feet of the protestors,' instructed Maguire.

'Does the good Professor have anything particular in mind?' said Dewhurst.

'Not really. That is up to yourselves. What you have to do is plan and organise yourselves to be on the look out for anything that can be used against the peaceniks to our advantage. For example, in the States we're hotting up the war of words against Libya in order to divert attention from the nuclear issue. But whatever you choose, the major criterion of acceptability is that it must originate here, in Britain. America must not be seen to have a hand in it. Otherwise you'll be wasting your time. Britain's position within the European Community will ensure that where Britain leads, the rest will follow. You, gentlemen, have to show the way.'

Harrogate, England

I

Sergeant Pickford already knew all the facts. But he still had to go through the formality of interviewing the neighbours. The residents of Beech Grove would expect the police to do that in the case of a violent death. He had saved Mrs Graham to the last because she, more than anyone else, had her finger on the pulse of what went on in the Grove. Her name was on file at headquarters.

She sat in her wheelchair gazing out of the bedroom window at the house opposite where Pickford's Special Branch partners were working. 'I knew it would happen again,' she mumbled. 'Just as it happened to me eighteen years ago. In the winter, those steps are a death trap. You only need a little bit of ice.'

Pickford had his notebook open but so far she hadn't told him anything new. 'When was the last time you saw him?'

'I can only see the bottom six steps from here,' she said, as if the policeman had not spoken. 'There are thirty-one altogether. They twist and turn up to Otley Road. I'm lucky to be alive. That's what the doctor told me.'

'Yes. I know. What . . .?'

'I was loaded down with Christmas shopping. Both arms full. I was at the top. I took one step. Then another.' She glanced at Pickford. 'Then I slipped. They found me at the bottom, unconscious. I fell all the way down.' Her voice was full of self-pity. She raked a bony claw through her greying hair and patted the bun at the back. 'If it was going to happen again, it was going to happen to him.' She nodded in the direction of the house across the road.

'Why's that?'

Mrs Graham turned her chair to face him. 'He had it written all over him. From the first day he moved in three years since.'

'Really? In what way?'

'He had a woman with him then. His wife I suppose. But she didn't stay long. He always came home with a brown paper bag tucked under his arm.' She stared at the policeman. 'Brandy,' she snorted. 'That's why she left.'

'You're sure it was brandy?' asked Pickford, facetiously.

'He dropped one of his paper bags one night. The bottle smashed on the pavement. Mrs Cardew swore it was brandy. That was just before the woman moved out. Then he started drinking more. He'd even sneak out at night to the off-licence to restock. Started carrying home his habit in cardboard boxes then. I don't know what kind of job he had, but he certainly used to take plenty of time off. And he didn't seem to have a set time for leaving or returning. Do you know where he worked?'

'I can't remember exactly,' replied Pickford. 'Somewhere close by, though.'

'But he never bothered anybody in the Grove. He kept very much to himself. Even when he came home drunk, staggering and falling all over the pavement, he never disturbed anybody. Not like that awful Mr Pertwee who lives that way.' She pointed with her thumb.

'So you think Mr Burton was drunk when he fell down the steps last night?'

'Well, he's been drunk every night for the past three years. Why should he have been sober last night? The post-mortem will confirm what I say. There's no doubt in my mind that he was drunk. And that was what killed him. That and those steps.'

Sergeant Pickford got to his feet. 'Thank you, Mrs Graham.'

'The evil of alcohol. Thank God I'm blessed with a husband who doesn't drink. He hasn't touched a drop since my accident.' She looked up at Pickford. 'He does everything for me. He's a wonderful man.'

'I'm sure he is, Mrs Graham.' Sergeant Pickford shook her hand. He had read her file before the interview. She had indeed been out shopping on the day of her accident. But she had neglected to mention the fact that on her way home she had stopped off at the local pub with her sister. Both women had tucked away several brandies. She had been drunk herself when she had taken the two fateful steps that had crippled her.

II

Burton paid off the taxi midway along Otley Road. Nike saw him scramble out, rummage through his pockets, then hand over a couple of notes to the driver, who snatched at them greedily then drove off before Burton, hand out ready for his change, realised he had gone.

Nike moved forward to the top of the steps and waited beneath the old-fashioned street lamp fastened to the wall, whose weak glow fought a losing battle against the heavy, wintry darkness. Burton reeled towards him, arms elbow-deep in his overcoat pockets, head bowed forward, unaware of Nike's presence. He collided with Nike then tried to push through him.

'Hello Burton,' said Nike, steadying the man with both

hands. Burton stepped back and looked up. There was no sign of recognition on his face. He blinked very slowly then moved forward again.

Nike shifted to one side, leaving a gap between himself and the wall, which Burton entered, placing his feet on the top step. Nike threw his left leg across his path and at the same time struck Burton with all his force behind the ear with a balled fist.

Burton sailed out over the first few steps, then crashed with a crunching thud against the stone. Nike watched the body, a twisting, grey blur, against the enclosed blackness, pitch and twist down the steps, until it disappeared round the bend.

He walked down Otley Road to collect the stolen car.

London, England

I

Maitland walked slowly. The trauma of his recent, brief imprisonment lingered on. Because his confinement had been so abrupt and unexpected, his release had brought on an exaggerated recognition of all that he had previously taken for granted. He felt like a child suddenly let loose in its favourite toy shop; incapable of taking in all that was on display. He walked slowly, to reaffirm his position in the great tramp of humanity, watching and listening.

He allowed himself to be jostled and pushed at the ticket barrier and to be swept along in the dash for the exit: he hadn't travelled by Tube for years and he luxuriated in the contacts his body made with fellow-travellers. He would do it more often, he told himself, as he emerged at Hyde Park Corner. The sun was not yet fully awake; it hid its face in embarrassment behind endless rows of grey, fluffy clouds. The morning air was sharp and brittle, needles of ice that stabbed at exposed skin. Pedestrians whose eccentric walks resembled wary ostriches puffed out smoke from invisible cigars. Shoes and boots crunched on frost-covered pavements. Cars and buses edged along the road, their drivers hypnotised by the slap of windscreen wipers, their passengers wrapped in layers of streaming hot air. Office windows beckoned the rush-hour crowds with dreary beacons of light, and porters hopped from foot to foot, arms swinging to and fro, dreaming of mugs of scalding tea.

Maitland perceived the world with a nascent awareness, dilated but acute.

II

'They told me downstairs you were back,' said Craig, as he burst into Maitland's office. He gave his friend a quick inspection. 'Your face,' he exclaimed. 'You look terrible.'

Maitland sat down carefully. His back was still painful. He didn't need reminding of his face: purple smudges under the hazel eyes, dark bruising on the cheekbone, a broken, scarred hairline. In contrast, Craig was manifestly brand new; his face was bright red, his eyes alive and shiny and his short hair was neatly and smoothly in place.

'It looks worse than it is, actually,' said Maitland casually.

'I'll bet,' said Craig, and winked knowingly. 'Anyway, the damage will be minor compared to what Capstick has in store for you. He's after your blood, Ollie.' He tried to perch on the edge of the desk, but his short legs would not afford him the necessary balance, so he wiggled his backside fully on to the top, leaving his feet swinging in mid-air.

'What happened? The Greenham women have a go at you?'

'No. It was the guardians of the law,' said Maitland sharply.

'Ollie, when Capstick told you to have a nose round Greenham, he didn't mean you were to join forces with the protestors and get it broken.' He grinned broadly. 'You were supposed to meet up with the surveillance team, take a couple of snapshots of the ringleaders, then head back to the office.'

'I know. But I wanted to have a proper look round to see what was going on, so I mingled with a group who were supporting the Greenham women's blockade.'

'And got duffed up.'

'A uniformed officer was punching a woman in the stomach,' said Maitland stiffly. 'He had her up against the fence, beating her like a punch bag.' He fingered the deep scratch on his chin, a red ribbon against the pale skin, and felt the bristles he had left unshaven around the wound. 'I intervened.' He flared his nostrils angrily.

'Come off it, Ollie. You've seen worse in Northern Ireland.'

'That's different. There's a war going on over there.'

'And over here, too.' Craig's voice had lost its banter.

'Against the women?'

'Against Soviet-inspired subversion.'

'Nonsense. There's nothing to show that these protests are orchestrated by the Kremlin. You know it. I know it. And those at the top know it.' Maitland stood up. 'Do you want to know how the trouble started? How I got myself arrested? An anti-peace campaign group calling themselves Peace Through Nuclear Strength started it all. They attacked the blockade and the police joined in with them.'

Craig did not reply. He gazed down at his feet which were neatly encased in black leather shoes.

Maitland continued, 'We've endless reports on the peace campaigners, but very little on this group. I looked them up this morning in the Archives. They're tied in with some of the more extreme groups in Europe and America. But we don't bother them. We leave them alone.'

'Look, Ollie. There's always been an extremist right-wing tradition in British political life. And in America. But it's always been kept under control.'

'Yes,' said Maitland, deep in thought. 'I wonder if von

44

Hindenburg said the same thing when he appointed Hitler as Chancellor in 1933?'

III

'Tragic, really,' said Maitland.

'Did you know him well?' asked Gregson. He was Capstick's deputy in F Branch and was standing in for him in his absence.

'He was my boss in Ireland. Nice chap. But the job got to him. Started drinking.' Maitland shrugged his shoulders. 'His work suffered as a result.'

'So he was given one of the famous promotions-demotions,' said Gregson wryly. 'Liaison Officer with the Americans at Menwith Hill.'

'His wife left him soon after they moved to Harrogate. He was working on the *Jumpseat* and *Chalet* satellite programmes. And I suppose it was all downhill from then on. Usual story.' Maitland got to his feet. He didn't want to talk further to Gregson, not after the dressing down he had received from him over the Greenham affair. He didn't need reminding of the weekend spent in prison after his fracas with the police, and the rather clumsily prolonged effort by Capstick to have him released.

Maitland realised that Gregson, a decent sort, was trying to soften the effect of the reprimand by gossiping, but Maitland did not think that Burton's sad demise was the most propitious subject for doing so.

'The autopsy says he was dead drunk at the time,' said Gregson. Maitland edged nearer the door, like an eager schoolboy anticipating the bell that would signal playtime. 'Accidental death according to the coroner. Broke his neck falling down some steps.' Gregson picked up the document and read to himself.

'Will that be all?' asked Maitland, his hand on the door knob.

Gregson waved him away.

Burton's death had saddened him. He wanted some time alone. He did not return to his office; instead he went out and crossed the road into Shepherd's Market. He needed a drink. Badly. The thought occurred to him later in the pub, as he drank his third whisky, that perhaps he was on the same slippery slope that had claimed Burton.

Witney, England

I

Thompson led the way into the library. Maitland thanked him as he closed the door.

'Ah! You've finally made it,' said Simon.

Maitland crossed to the french windows. 'How are you, Simon?'

'I am very well my boy. And you?' He pumped his nephew's hand vigorously. 'Julia not with you?'

'Fine. Fine. I'm sorry I really couldn't get away any sooner. And Julia was called in to work at the last moment.'

'That's a pity.' Simon sounded disappointed.

Maitland looked around. 'Where's everybody else?'

Simon relinquished his handhold and then attacked Maitland's shoulder with a series of avuncular pats. 'They didn't bring your mother down to lunch.' Maitland grimaced. 'Not to worry, Ollie. She seems fine. She was sleeping at the time. Thought it best not to disturb her. Jane's up with her now.'

'Not much of a birthday party for the old girl,' said Maitland sadly. 'Glad you made it though,' he added fondly.

'Never fail. And I'm pleased you did too. You've missed lunch but we saved some birthday cake for you.' He grinned impishly at Maitland. 'How about a drink?'

Maitland poured himself a whisky and topped up his uncle's glass. 'And where is the lord of the manor?'

'Your father?' Simon shrugged his shoulders. 'I don't know. Probably in the kitchen hanging a couple of servants. The soup was only lukewarm.' He raised his voice in imitation of his brother-in-law. 'This lamb is stringy.'

Maitland laughed. 'If he's in one of those moods, I'd better steer clear of him.'

'Me too,' Simon agreed, gulping down his drink. 'I suggested he should only keelhaul the offenders in the lake. Didn't like that one bit. Come on. Let's go for a walk. Can't waste a nice day like this skulking indoors.' He stepped out onto the patio with Maitland in attendance.

II

They climbed the steps to the gazebo. Maitland sniffed the air. 'Phew,' he snorted.

'It's the *dragon arums*,' said his uncle, pointing to an array of tall, maroon flowers at the bend in the border. 'They begin to smell after a few days in bloom. They attract flies which act as pollinators.'

'Not the best place to plant them,' said Maitland. They sat on a wooden bench in silence.

'Is that all, then?' said Simon eventually.

'I don't know, uncle.' He ran his fingers through his hair. 'At school there was a chap who was the biggest sneak and snitch I ever met. He wore a path through the carpet leading to the housemaster's study. We made his life hell. But that didn't stop him. He carried on regardless.'

'Some boys are like that, Oliver.'

'I know. Every school has one. I'm feeling rather like one myself at the moment.'

'A sneak and a snitch?'

'Yes. Looking into people's mail. Listening in on what they say. Ordinary men and women going about their business. And then making reports, filing them away for later use. It makes me sick.'

'It was your choice to go into the Security Service, Oliver,' said Simon quietly.

'I know. I know. You said politics. Father wanted me in the Army. Mother wanted me in the Diplomatic Corps. I thought, well, if it's the Corps, father would have made mother's life even more of a misery. And the Army would have disappointed her. I chose the Service because you . . .'

'You liked Northern Ireland, didn't you?' interrupted Simon.

'Yes. That's what I mean. I was doing something positive. Admittedly it was undercover. But . . .'

'But your father didn't think so?'

'You were here. The Christmas before last, remember?' He imitated his father's booming voice. 'You should be a soldier if you're in Ireland.'

'I remember. And you think he had something to do with your transfer?'

'Not something. All. Transferred to the Counter-subversion Branch,' he said disgustedly.

'Shush. I'm not supposed to know.'

'To hell with it. Eighteen bloody months of listening at keyholes. It's driving me crazy.'

'I don't think you'll be there much longer,' said Simon casually. 'Not from what your father said over lunch.'

'What? He wouldn't . . .'

'Auntie Jane ate lunch upstairs in your mother's room. She didn't like your father's mood. So it was him and I alone.'

'What did he say?'

49

'Just a few broad hints. Mainly about you not getting on in your Department. Talking too much. Out of turn mostly.'

'He said that?'

'He's angry with you, Oliver. I think you might have embarrassed him.'

'The man's too thick-skinned for that.'

'True.' Simon was staring at the floor. 'He hasn't called to see your mother for over a month, you know. Up till today, that is. I doubt if he's seen her today, either. He arrived in a rush, spoke to the nurse, then ordered up lunch.'

'Mother's always been a liability to him in his estimation.'

III

'Well, Oliver. They must be working you very hard indeed for you to miss your mother's birthday lunch.' They stood facing each other in the study, the short distance between them the chasm of *San Luis Rey*. Both men were the same height, two inches over six feet, straight backed, lean and lithe, and their hair and eye colour was the same. But where Oliver's hazel eyes sparkled, his father's were dull and hooded.

Sir Samuel Frederick Maitland sat down in his leather armchair without proffering a welcoming hand to his son. He crossed his legs, inspected the crease in his blue trousers and shot his cuffs. Oliver remained standing. Sunbeams danced across his father's shoulders, and reflected from the polished wood of the oak bookcases and the French walnut desk. The smell of old leather, shiny and cracked, worn with age, pervaded the room, screening the faint mustiness of the threadbare rugs and the dust-laden curtains.

'Have you been up to see mother, yet?' said Oliver.

'I will call on her before I leave this evening.'

'And if she sleeps through?'

His father ignored the question. 'I am not happy at all, Oliver, with the way you are progressing.'

'Am I on the carpet, Father?'

'Don't be cheeky, young man,' he snapped.

Oliver sat down in the chair by the fireside and stared into the empty grate.

'How old are you now? Almost thirty? And look at you. No thought of marriage. No interest in the firm. And causing trouble in your Department.'

Maitland was reminded of the argument he had with Craig just after his visit to Greenham Common, and the run-ins with his Departmental Head, James Capstick. Then there was the firm. His father's firm. Offices in London and New York. The Maitland Trust. A money machine. In polite conversation his father was referred to as a dealer or a broker. He bought and sold large companies and small conglomerates all over the world. In less polite circles, he was called an asset-stripper, while some of his business dealings had left him with the sobriquet of robber baron. He was well known and respected in the City, and on more than one occasion had advised the government on financial matters both at home and abroad. His whole life, after service in the army, had been dedicated to the love and pursuit of money.

'Have you nothing to say for yourself?'

'At Eton, Jack Craig wore a hole in the carpet . . .'

'Craig's a fine young man. Know his father well. We were knighted in the same Honours List.'

'. . . leading to the housemaster's study. I thought he'd changed.'

Sir Samuel crashed his fist down onto the desk. 'He's not the problem! It's you!' He jabbed a finger at Maitland. 'You're the problem. Causing trouble with your colleagues and superiors. I didn't want you in the Service in the first place. But now that you're in you'll stay there until you are a success.'

'I was a success. In Northern Ireland.'

'That cesspit is a job for the Army. It's here, in England, in London, where you should be.'

'Did you have to pull the strings very hard to get me moved?'

'You're going to move again. On and up. You're going to work hard. Damn hard. And you're going to keep your childish prattle to yourself. You've caused me a great deal of embarrassment among certain of my friends. And it'll be a long time before I forgive you for that.' He got to his feet and came to stand over his son. 'When I can speak your name with some pride, when I can point you out to my friends and tell them how well you are serving your country, then I'll forgive you. What on earth do you think your mother would say if she knew all about this?'

IV

'Where's Jane?' asked Moira Maitland weakly.

'It's all right,' whispered Maitland. 'She's gone downstairs to see Simon.'

'Is that you, Ollie?'

'Yes.' He held her hand. It was thin and pale, highlighting the blue of the veins. 'Who did you think it was?'

She closed her eyes. 'You look so much like your father.' She tried to sit up, but Maitland stopped her. She smiled at him and opened her eyes.

'How are you? I brought you a present. But I left it in the car.'

'Never mind.' She patted the back of his hand. 'You look pale, Ollie. Was it that bad? Father, I mean. Jane told me you had been invited into the study.'

Now Maitland patted her hand. Sir Samuel's study was his private preserve; not even mother was allowed entry unbidden. Sir Samuel issued invitations for one reason only. As a child, Maitland had witnessed his mother emerging from the room, ashen and trembling, while he himself had received some of the worst beatings of his life in that cold study. But from the age of eleven, he had resolved never to show his father any tears, any fear, any pain. He had borne his thrashings stoically like a repentant sinner, surprising his father with his fortitude. 'No,' he replied with a laugh. 'Just the usual tirade.'

'Oh, Ollie. What are we going to do?' She was dying. The doctors said a cancer: Maitland believed a broken heart. 'Why didn't you follow uncle Henry's advice?'

'Let's not go into that now, mother.'

'All that cloak and dagger business. It can't be good for you. The Somerville's never had such dealings.' Her family had come to Britain at the time of the Norman Conquest, from the village of Graveron-Somerville, and the family tree was well endowed with scholars and diplomats.

'But I'm a Maitland,' he teased. Maitland, he thought, from the French, *maltalent*, an ill-mannered man. How appropriate.

'Never,' she said with passion, and squeezed his hand. 'Your roots are here. In this house.'

She had been born in the house, as had several generations of Somervilles. She had brought it, together with a small legacy, to the marriage. Sir Samuel had exploited both, after securing a son and heir at the first attempt, in

53

his dogged, rapacious quest for wealth. Very early on in the marriage, it had become apparent to her that he did not consider the house his home, his absences becoming more prolonged, with greater frequency.

His mother had resigned herself to the situation. She had not employed a nanny, preferring to devote all her time to her son's upbringing. She had wanted other children, but they were denied to her by Sir Samuel who had deemed them unnecessary. Maitland doubted that his father even kept a change of clothing in the house now.

'I understand,' said Maitland.

Her head lolled on the pillow. 'I'm going back to the hospital on Tuesday. Will you visit? And bring Julia?'

'I promise.' She closed her eyes. He leant forward and stroked her cheek. The skin was thin and paper-like, almost transparent. He kissed her on the brow and gently touched her hair. It was white now, what little there was left, coarse and lifeless. For a moment he saw her as he remembered her from his youth; rich auburn hair swept away from the forehead, animated brown eyes, firm, strong legs that were always on the move. He could not accept that this skeletal shell in the bed was his mother. He found it difficult to attend her.

London, England

Mercer was late. He rode the taxi down Curzon Street and right up to the main entrance of MI5 Headquarters. He paid, climbed out and dashed inside. It took five minutes for his security clearance to the fifth floor, and he arrived at the Director-General's office fifteen minutes beyond the appointed time.

'Go straight in, Mr Mercer,' said Peter Warner, rising to meet him. 'You're expected. And you're late.'

'I know. I know.' Mercer tucked his briefcase under his left arm and knocked firmly on the door before entering.

'Ah. You're wrong, Jimmy. MI6 do have some manners,' said the Director.

Mercer approached the ornate, wooden table around which the six men sat. 'Sorry I'm late. Traffic.' He sat in the only available chair.

'And Sir Peter?' asked the Director.

'Called away at the last moment. Foreign Office.'

'How inconvenient.' The Director tapped the table with a pen. 'Well then, Joseph. Down to business. We have other things to talk about that do not need the presence of MI6.'

'Yes. I understand.' Mercer began to open his briefcase.

Jimmy Capstick spoke. 'You've seen the transcripts of the latest interrogations?' Mercer nodded yes as he continued to unload his briefcase. 'And?'

Mercer paused in his work as he became aware of six pairs of eyes staring at him. 'And what?' he asked.

'Tell us what you think,' said Gregson who had handled the entire defection and debriefing.

'But I have told you.' Mercer began to rummage through the folders he had placed on the table. 'Two years ago. When you first went after Gouzenko. Very low-level member of *Glavnoye Razvedyvatelnoye Upravlenie*, the Intelligence Directorate of the Soviet General Staff.' He found what he was looking for. He held it up. 'My memo stating that he would be of no use to ourselves is dated two years ago. Do you remember?'

'And what about all the information in the transcripts?' asked Capstick.

Mercer began his search again. 'No less than four memos on those transcripts. The information they contained could have been picked out of the *Guardian*, the *New Statesman* or the *New York Times*. Wouldn't even classify it as low-grade intelligence. His whole background, slow promotion rate, his postings, all told me he wouldn't do. The transcripts confirmed that. I advised your people against bringing him out of Holland. And against wasting your time in a fruitless schedule of debriefings.'

'Oleg Gouzenko is an important member of the GRU,' persisted Capstick. 'He has provided MI5 with valuable information on their undercover activities in Holland and other EEC countries, including Britain.'

'Not according to what he's told you during the interrogations. What you think you've learnt over the last two years from Gouzenko has been on record in Century House for a decade.'

'Rubbish,' shouted Gregson.

'Russia Section staff have been over every word he's uttered since you brought him in. They thought it was some joke or other. They think you've been had.'

'Now look here, Mercer . . .'

'All right, Jimmy,' said the Director. 'I can see, Mr Mercer, why Sir Peter did not put in an appearance.'

Mercer's face went dark red. He pointed at the telephone. 'Committee room 3. Pick it up and ask for him.'

'Yes. Well.' The Director turned away from Mercer's angry glare. 'I take it that there will be no finance either from your Secret Vote or the Supplementary to care for our defector?'

'That is correct. We want nothing to do with Mr Gouzenko,' replied Mercer.

'So MI5 is to carry all the expenses?' asked Capstick.

'As the Director said, he is your defector.' Mercer collected up his paperwork.

'Don't be cheeky, Mercer,' said the Director forcefully. 'It won't be the first time either that we have proved you wrong. Gouzenko will pay dividends. Wait and see.' He dismissed Mercer with a wave of his hand, like a man swatting at a troublesome insect.

Mercer was about to speak. Instead he stood up. MI6 traditionally held MI5 in disdain. He had heard it described as the contempt that a guards' Officers Mess usually reserves for that of the military police. Sir Peter Ralston, Director of MI6, regarded the inmates of Curzon Street as unimaginative bureaucrats, comparable to the civil servants of Hitler's Reich, with their emphasis on form-filling and information storage. Mercer was inclined to agree. 'Thank you,' he said and left the room.

'Bastard,' swore Jimmy Capstick. 'Tight-fisted bastard.'

'What did you expect, Jimmy?' asked Gregson. 'An open cheque? You know where Mercer stands. Somewhere to the left of Josef Stalin.'

A few polite laughs greeted this attempt at humour, but Capstick would not be mollified. 'He'd say no if we brought him Andropov. It's always been the same. We bring someone in, and M I6 won't touch them.'

'True, Jimmy. But perhaps Mercer has a point over the Gouzenko case. I haven't seen anything from him that would make me want to fork out large sums of money for protection, new identity, a house. Have you?'

Capstick looked at the Director. 'I have a feeling about Gouzenko. Had it ever since the defection was first mooted. He'll come good.'

'Saving up the best bits to the end, perhaps?' Dewhurst had spoken. He had taken off his horn-rimmed spectacles and was polishing them slowly with a pale blue handkerchief. 'I don't think so, though. He's told us all he knows.'

The Director was almost deferential when he replied to his Head of Operations. 'Is that the way you see it, Alan?'

'Yes it is, Robert. Mercer was quite correct in his summation and his refusal to assist in the financing. We will have to carry that burden. Or rather I will. I want Mr Gouzenko. I have something for him to do.'

Shrewsbury, England

Thomas Roger March was a burglar. He was also a wife-beater.

'So I says, *I'll be home at seven for my dinner*. Well, then I met a few of the lads, and that was it until midnight. Had a few drinks,' explained March. 'I eventually get in about one, and the wife is sitting up waiting for me. You know, that martyred look on her face. So before she can start, I ask her where my dinner is. Get in first, see.'

'I see,' said Maitland. He kept his eyes on the road.

'*And it had better be hot*, I tell her. Well, she looks at me and says: *Of course it's hot; it's been on the back of the fire for the past two hours*. So I let her have it. Punched her in the mouth. Knocked out four teeth.'

'Did you go to prison for that?'

'No,' said March with a grin. 'I was on contract to you lot by then. Local police get the word to leave you alone. Know what I mean?' He nudged Maitland in the side and winked. 'I've never been inside.'

Maitland had had enough. Three hours with March was beyond the call of duty. He hadn't stopped talking since they had met up that morning. Maitland had heard it all, from small-time thief in the back streets of Birmingham, through to expert burglar in the West End of London. Then his recruitment into AIA section of Operations Branch of MI5, followed by a detailed list of all the burglaries he had performed in the service of his country.

59

'Any sign yet?' asked March.

'I thought you said about half-ten.'

'I did.'

'It's only quarter past,' said Maitland.

Maitland's transfer, dictated by his father, had come through very swiftly. Dewhurst had personally welcomed him into the fold. Maitland had towered above the man in his office, but Dewhurst had given him the impression that he relished the difference in height. It was as if he was already contemplating the various means he would employ to chop him down to size. And it was during that unaugural chat that Maitland had met Nike.

Dewhurst had been outlining some of the duties of an officer in the Operations Branch, A Branch as he referred to it, when suddenly a chill had raced down his spine. He had turned in his seat and his heart had skipped a beat. Standing directly behind him had been Nike. Maitland had not heard him enter the room. Dewhurst had not introduced him, but that had been unnecessary. Since his return to London, he had heard all he wanted to know about Dewhurst's factotum. Now he understood the rumours: there was a cold, rock-like stillness about the man, in his huge head and jutting chin, in the broad shoulders and large hands, but manifesting itself most frighteningly in the blank, immobile eyes.

'Nervous?' asked March.

Maitland realized he had been nervously drumming his fingers on his knees. 'No, just impatient.'

'Won't be long now,' said March. 'And remember. Don't rush. Act casual like. We're from the estate agents if anybody asks.'

Maitland thanked him for the uncalled for advice. He wasn't nervous. He was angry. He knew only too well why he had been sent up to Shrewsbury to supervise this operation. 'I want you there personally. Inside the house,' Dewhurst had said. Inside. Involved in this nasty burglary, so that he could get his hands dirty like everyone else in A Branch. He could still see the smug look on Dewhurst's face as he had spelt out his instructions.

'There she is. Bang on time.' March got out of the car. Maitland picked up the briefcase and followed him. 'Mrs Phizaclea is the next-door neighbour. Nosey old bitch. But regular as clockwork with her morning shopping.'

Maitland wore a pin-striped business suit, white shirt and a tie. March was dressed almost identically. They passed Mrs Phizaclea on the corner of Sutton Road. She said good morning. Both men returned the greeting.

Mrs Phizaclea lived at number 42. They strolled past her house and turned into the drive of the one next door. There was a *For Sale* board on a post just inside the gateway. The house was empty. The owner, Mrs Hilda Green, a widow, was away for the week, staying with her son in Plymouth. The house had been up for sale for a month now.

March strode up to the front door with a bunch of keys in his hand. It took him a second or two to gain entry. He held the door open for Maitland to enter, then closed it firmly behind him.

'Back bedroom,' said March, pointing to the stairs. 'That's where she usually burns the midnight oil.'

Maitland went upstairs. March had kept Mrs Green and her house under surveillance for some time now, and he knew all about the woman's habits. The back bedroom would be the most likely place to find her report.

But the room was empty. All that was there was a table, a chair and a covered typewriter. No typescripts, notes or reference books. Nevertheless, he searched the room. He went downstairs and found March in the lounge reading a woman's magazine.

'Nothing there,' he reported.

March stood up. 'Let's take a nose about.'

They searched the house from top to bottom, but could find nothing. The more they looked, the more irritated March became. Maitland suspected that March had been careless during his surveillance and that Mrs Green had spotted him and cleared everything out of the house. Maitland's impression of the old woman, from MI5's *still life* of her, was that of an intelligent, shrewd and canny individual. March, in his dismissive disregard for all punters, had probably underestimated her.

Finally, March decided that it was time to get out. They had been inside too long: Mrs Phizaclea would be back soon. An unusually quiet and downcast March led the way out.

Maitland was glad of the silence on the drive back to London. He was glad too that they had not found Mrs Green's report. His hands were not too dirty: he hadn't stolen anything. MI5 would have to wait for a copy of Mrs Green's report, on the link between the civil nuclear industry and the armament corporations, until she circulated it among the peace movement.

London, England

I

'What do you know about the *Spetsnaz*?' asked Dewhurst.

'*Spetsnaz*?' said Maitland, and he frowned in concentration.

'You've read the Gouzenko transcripts?'

'Yes.'

'Well?' prompted Dewhurst.

'Sounds familiar.' Maitland stroked his chin. Dewhurst took off his glasses and began to polish them on his handkerchief. Dewhurst's fingers reminded Maitland of uncooked chipolata sausages, pinky-white, cylindrical, tight-skinned. He was mesmerised by their slow, deliberate movements, and hypnotic motion, that gave the impression that they had a separate identity from their owner.

'The Semichastny proposal?' hinted Dewhurst. He put on his spectacles.

'Oh yes, I remember now.' Maitland snapped out of his trance. 'The *Spetsnaz*. An elite body of troops. Similar to our SAS. Semichastny recommended their formation. They were used to infiltrate the West. But his proposal was never acted upon according to Gouzenko.'

'Thank you, Mr Maitland.' Dewhurst tugged the ends of his waistcoat over his rounded paunch and folded his arms. The waistcoat crept up again to expose the tips of his braces. 'But Gouzenko could be mistaken. The *Spetsnaz* could have been recruited and trained without his knowledge.'

Maitland was unconvinced. 'Perhaps. He only mentions them once or twice in relation to the proposal which was made over twenty years ago. Then nothing more.'

'Twenty years is a long time. Perhaps Mr Gouzenko was too busy elsewhere to concern himself with the *Spetsnaz*.'

'From his position inside the GRU, I doubt very much that such a force could have been formed without Gouzenko hearing about it.'

'Nevertheless, I am of the opinion that the *Spetsnaz* exist,' said Dewhurst forcefully. 'And that they pose a great danger to Britain and Europe.' He sat forward. 'I have a task for you, Oliver. A very important one. I want you to help Mr Gouzenko to write his memoirs. About the *Spetsnaz* in particular.'

II

Maitland took the tube to Regent's Park and walked up Albany Street to the barracks. The SAS maintained a permanent force in London, attached to the Special Branch, a rapid deployment troop whose task was to combat acts of terrorism in the capital.

He showed his documentation several times, was frisked twice, then photographed, before being shown to a room on the fourth floor, where he was greeted by a young man with a wispy moustache, dressed in a dark tweed jacket, grey slacks, white shirt and Royal Artillery tie. He didn't give his name. Nor did he offer Maitland any refreshment.

'My CO doesn't want these manuals to leave here,' said the SAS man.

'I don't particularly want to take them. But I have my orders. As does your CO,' replied Maitland.

The man nibbled the corner of his moustache. 'Got anything to carry them in?'

'You are to provide a metal security box,' said Maitland in a bored voice. 'A car and an escort. Read the orders.'

He cropped the opposite end of the moustache before replying, 'The SAS manual is all you'll need, actually.'

Maitland held up his hand and counted off his fingers. 'SAS Training Manual. Special Boat Squadron. French Paratroopers. The German GSG-9 manual. The Israeli Squad 101.' He transferred to the other hand. 'Finally, the American Delta Force manual. Six of them. As requested.'

'The Delta Force manual won't be of much use. When the Yanks formed that unit, their commander spent three months over here with us. Then he took six of our boys back to Fort Bragg for ten weeks to set up their training programme. So it'll all be in ours.'

'Can I take the manuals now? Including the Delta Force,' said Maitland as if he hadn't heard the man. 'I am in rather a hurry.' Maitland didn't expect the moustache to recover from the trauma of the meeting.

III

'Come in Oliver. You know Mike Maguire? CIA Station Head.' Dewhurst beckoned him forward to the long table on which were spread a jumble of maps and photographs.

'Yes. We've met before.' He shook hands with Maguire.

'Nice to see you again, Oliver,' said Maguire. He had huge hands, like shovels, and the hairs on them were thick and wiry.

'Gouzenko not with you?' enquired Dewhurst.

'He's taken to working through the night and sleeping during the day.'

'Is he making progress?' said Maguire.

Maitland nodded. 'Fair. But he's not very pleased with Tompkins.'

'Tompkins?' said Maguire.

'Service Intelligence. Russian military expert,' said Dewhurst. 'What's the problem?'

'Personality clash, perhaps. Tompkins says his home life is suffering. Gouzenko says Tompkins works him too hard. Who knows.'

'Now they can cut out that bullshit,' said Maguire angrily. 'That *Spetsnaz* book has got to be ready for galley-proofs in six months' time. How many manuals have they done?'

'They're still on the first one. The SAS manual.'

'That's not good enough,' said Dewhurst.

'Damn right it's not, Alan. I'm going to have to go down there and kick ass.'

Maitland felt the onset of a grin in his lips. 'It is three times as large as any of the others. And the most detailed.' He looked at the floor.

'Yes. I'm sure it is. Once that one is out of the way, progress will improve?' Dewhurst suggested.

'I'm sure it will.'

'Make sure they read the Delta Force Manual next,' said Maguire.

'As you wish,' said Maitland.

'And keep me up to date with how things are going. Weekly. We've got a deadline to keep.'

'I know.'

'Right, Oliver,' purred Dewhurst. 'Take a look at these, will you?' Dewhurst walked round the table. He shoved some of the chaos aside and spread out a large-scale map of the Soviet Union. 'In the north. Here.' He tapped the area covered by the Arctic Ocean. 'Wrangle Island. Off the coast of Khabarovsk. The GRU's finishing school. Then there's the Sanprobal Military Academy in the Crimea. Another GRU camp. And then in the Ukraine, the Higher Infantry School in Odessa.'

'All mentioned in the Gouzenko transcripts,' said Maguire. 'The last named is jointly run by the KGB and the GRU. The three of them are specialised training centres. That is where the *Spetsnaz* will train.'

Maitland nodded. Dewhurst was being Mr Nice today, letting Maguire do all the harassing. 'Will there be any photographs?'

'Spy-in-the-sky.' Dewhurst extracted several large prints from a stack at the edge of the table. 'Mike brought them over today.' He put one in front of Maitland, lowered the table-light and handed him a magnifying glass. '*KH-2* satellite picture of Wrangle Island. Last year, Mike?'

'About then. You can see the camp layout very clearly. What we're going to do is blow it up a bit more, get one of your artists to make one or two changes, add one or two structures, and bingo. The main training camp of the *Spetsnaz*.'

Maitland studied the print. It didn't look very clear to him. But he had no doubt that when it was included in Gouzenko's book detailing the history, training and deployment of the *Spetsnaz*, it would do the job it was supposed to do.

'We've others for the Crimea and Ukraine centres. Now. Personnel. We have . . .'

IV

Vernon Kell, a captain in the Staffordshire regiment during the Great War, was instructed by his superiors to set up Military Intelligence Department 5. His brief was to provide misleading information to German agents positioned inside Britain who were spying on the British war effort. Kell was so successful at his task that his group, MI5, was placed under the aegis of the Home Office when the war ended. The task of MI5 was to provide counter-intelligence against the increasing menaces of Bolshevism and Fascism. Kell, or K as he was to become known inside MI5, stayed on as Director-General until his dismissal in 1940.

Major General Sir Vernon Kell is generally credited with giving the world of espionage its most potent weapon, disinformation: the spreading or placing of false and misleading information with the enemy in order to confuse and deceive the enemy as to the author's true intention.

Borough High Street was where Maitland had learnt all about disinformation techniques. His mind tried to conjure up an image of the place but the intrusion of the bickering going on next door made it impossible. The level of the noise was rising steadily and he knew that in a very short time he would have to forgo his reverie and mediate again between Gouzenko and Tompkins.

He heard a door slam and footsteps descending. Reluctantly he rose from the bunk bed and went to see what had happened.

Gouzenko sat at his table surrounded by a pile of papers and the training manuals. He looked up sheepishly as Maitland entered. Johnstone and Myers were standing by the window. 'Go and get him,' ordered Maitland. The two men quickly left. 'What was that one over?' he asked Gouzenko.

Gouzenko gave a Gallic shrug. 'That silly man. He won't listen to me. He always wants . . .'

'Okay. Okay,' said Maitland. He pulled up a chair next to Gouzenko. He sighed wearily.

'You look tired, Mr Maitland,' said Gouzenko.

Maitland stifled a yawn. 'You don't look exactly full of life yourself. There's too much work to be done to worry about the luxury of rest and sleep.'

'I wonder if it's the amount of work, or the work itself, that is responsible for the fatigue.' Gouzenko did not look at Maitland as he spoke.

When Maitland did not reply, Gouzenko continued. 'My father had a penchant for quoting the words of Adolf Hitler. Chapter ten of *Mein Kampf* was his favourite, particularly this little gem. "*The great masses of the people will more easily fall victims to a great lie than to a small one.*" Do you recognize it?'

'Yes. Plato said as much in the *Republic*. Over two thousand years before Hitler was born.'

'Hitler was a plagiarist among his other attributes,' said Gouzenko. 'But what I never understood about my father was why he quoted Hitler. And then one day, not long after I had joined the GRU, it came to me. He was warning me. In a roundabout fashion. He was telling me to beware of the monstrous distortions that the Russian leaders made of the facts. To the Kremlin, truth is the hostage of the Party and the State.'

'Is that why you defected? To get away from that?' asked Maitland.

'Yes. And here I am . . .' He gestured at the training manuals in front of him.

Maitland was staring off into space.

Oxford, England

I

'You never ever told mother you once worked for MI5, did you?' said Maitland.

'No. Why do you ask?' said Simon.

Maitland slowed the car as they approached the traffic lights. 'Oh. Just something she said recently.' He braked as the lights turned red. They were on the way back from the hospital. 'Why have you never told her?'

Simon scratched his head. In the dark his white hair and beard glinted with silver. 'I don't know, really. I'm a lot older than your mother. She was just a girl when the war broke out. I told her I worked for the Ministry of Supply. She has always looked upon me as a bit of an old fuddy-duddy whose only interest in life was burrowing my way through ancient scripts and texts. I suppose I didn't want to disillusion her.'

'That was father's prerogative,' said Maitland sadly. He accelerated away on green. His mother was coming out the following day. There had been a remission. The doctors said she could go home. Maitland had travelled up to Oxford on one of his infrequent visits and had met Simon there. 'Bletchley Park, wasn't it. Codes and Ciphers?'

'Don't tell me they still have me on file?'

'I looked you up in the Archives just after I joined. They have everything down there. Right back to day one and old Vernon Kell.'

'My time there was most enjoyable. I made some good

friends there. After the War, I was liaison officer with MI6. But it's a lot different now I'll bet.'

'It has to be. During the war you knew for certain who the enemy was. But today. Well, you don't know for sure.'

'Knowing your enemy is not the primary consideration. You have to know what you are defending first of all. Then the enemy will show itself.'

II

Simon had persuaded his nephew to stay overnight: in the morning, they would return to the hospital to collect his mother.

'Come in, dear boy. Come in,' said Simon. He ushered Maitland into the tiny living room of his *pied à terre*. 'I have rooms up at the College,' he explained. 'But they are a little impersonal. This is where I keep all my treasures.'

The room seemed small because it was stacked from floor to ceiling with books and scripts which had encroached upon most of the available space, so that only a single, narrow track across the floor remained. Maitland trod warily, eyeing the ill-balanced accumulations, as he followed his uncle into the unknown.

'Take a seat, Oliver,' said his uncle. He indicated one of two misshapen armchairs whose bottoms had gone, marooned in the centre of the room, like two broken-down camels. 'I'll get something to drink. Cocoa? Or would you prefer something stronger?'

'Cocoa's fine,' said Maitland. He wondered if his uncle was ever bothered by claustrophobia.

'What were you saying earlier?' asked Simon from the kitchen. His voice was partially lost amongst the rattle of pans and the slamming of cupboard doors.

'I wasn't saying anything. I was listening,' shouted Maitland.

'That's right,' said Simon, as he popped his head round the door. 'Won't be a minute.' The head retreated but the voice remained. 'Since the war, the power and wealth of the armaments corporations has grown exponentially.'

Maitland only half listened. He was dog tired. The work with Gouzenko was grinding him down as it had done Tompkins. But it was nearing completion. He rubbed his eyes and rested his head on the back of the chair. It was rock hard. There was one consolation to his involvement with Gouzenko: it meant he couldn't be dragged in to the campaign MI5 was currently waging against the miners and Arthur Scargill. Dewhurst's task took priority.

'Are you listening?' said Simon. He stood over Maitland with a cup of steaming cocoa in each hand. 'Here. I think this is yours?'

Maitland took the cup, which burnt his fingers before they found the handle. 'Thanks. Cheers.' As he raised it to his lips, he could smell brandy. 'I think this is yours,' he added after taking a sip. He pulled a face. They swopped cups.

'A trick I learnt at Bletchley. Brandy and cocoa. Guarantees a deep sleep without snoring. You should try it.'

'This is fine.'

Simon rested his cup on his knee. 'Hundreds of thousands of men and women are employed in the manufacture of weapons, particularly the nuclear ones. Some of the best brains in the world are involved in the research. Billions and billions of dollars are involved.'

'I know, Simon,' said Maitland. He yawned, but it went unnoticed. He'd forgotten who had first broached the subject of power and high finance: it was one of Simon's favourites, one he never tired of. The topic usually arose in connection with Maitland's father who was always discussed whenever they were together.

Simon continued. 'The West needs nuclear armaments for its own economic well-being. In the West, capitalism is the ultimate arbiter. For the Soviet bloc it is ideology. The greatest threat the Russians pose to us would be to sue for peace. It is not in the financial interests of the West to disarm.'

Maitland saw that Simon was becoming very animated. He dashed to the kitchen and returned with the bottle of brandy. Maitland refused the offer. Simon poured a stiff one into his cocoa.

'Questions of defence don't enter into it then?' said Maitland.

'The armaments lobby is very powerful, its propaganda most persuasive. Some politicians truly believe the message that the West can only stave off the menace of Russia by a show of nuclear strength. Others can see through the propaganda, but pay it lip service because they realize the economic connections and implications.'

Maitland smiled broadly at his uncle. 'Really, Simon?'

'Don't scoff, my dear boy,' said Simon. 'Politicians may sound convincing, but in trying to convince us, the public, they also convince themselves and become victims of the propaganda. I have never considered suicide as a sane defence strategy.'

Simon's head tended to wobble whenever he was making a point, as if the movement helped to shake his thoughts into a logical sequence, and as it bobbed to and fro, wayward strands of his thin, white hair looped down across his brow like filaments of wire escaping from a roll of wire wool.

'You old lefty, you,' said Maitland affectionately.

'It stands to reason. Prompted by expanding, innovative

73

technologies, new weapons have to be developed and deployed, old ones scrapped, if the technological and economical cycles are to continue, if the military-industrial complex is to survive. It is not a question of defence at all.'

'Risky business,' said Maitland drowsily.

'True enough,' said Simon. 'Very risky indeed. But where there are big risks there are also huge profits. To the captains of the armaments industry, a nuclear warhead and its delivery system is simply a saleable commodity. Just like a car or a washing machine. At the end of the day, it is the profit column on the balance sheet that is of paramount importance.'

'That is a highly cynical view of our world.'

'Perhaps. But the possibility that the world could be blown to smithereens does not matter to these industrialists. It is not the gun that kills but the person holding it. Similarly, it is not the bomb that will bring about the holocaust, but the person who presses the button.'

Maitland sat up and grinned. 'No, Simon. The question of morality does not arise? The balance sheet is all important? Surely not.'

'Where profits are concerned there can be no morality. Ask your father.'

INTERLUDE

1985

Brighton, England

The student revolt of the late sixties and early seventies that developed simultaneously in America, Europe and Britain, was responsible for bringing Alan Harold Dewhurst to the attention of his superiors.

During that time Dewhurst infiltrated that student movement with a small band of MI5 officers, and a motley mob of rogues and reprobates whose only loyalty was to the hand that fed them. These *agents provocateurs*, on Dewhurst's instructions, orchestrated and led the terrible violence that convulsed the peaceful student protest. Ultimately, the movement was discredited in the eyes of the public and eventually faded into oblivion. In contrast, Dewhurst rose to prominence, the nick-name *Butcher* an accolade he wore with pride, a reminder to the younger generation of MI5 of how he had won his spurs.

Within the Security Service he was seen as a necessary evil, the man who was charged with all the ugly, underhand business that was known to go on, but which the minority of more sensitive and altruistic officers of the Service preferred to believe was not taking place. In the corridors of Whitehall and Westminster, Dewhurst's presence brought on an arctic chill, and Ministers and their staff kept contact to a minimum, abnegating their responsibilities, allowing Dewhurst a free hand, in the hope he would depart and leave them alone.

So when Dewhurst called for the briefing session, the response was rapid.

Seven men and two women from the Home Office and the Ministry of Defence faced him in the tiny lecture hall inside the MI5 training complex that overlooked the sea on the south coast. He had been given one day to pass on his wishes and instructions.

'Some of you were involved in the last Home Defence exercise, *Square Leg*, in 1980. All of you are currently engaged in the preliminary planning for the next one, *Brave Defender*, scheduled to take place in the autumn of 1985.' Dewhurst noticed some confusion among his audience.

'I'm sorry, Mr Dewhurst, but we were informed that this briefing concerned the Bernhardt Memorandum,' said one of the women.

Dewhurst read her name from the tag pinned above her right breast. Mary Masitter. 'That is correct,' he said dismissively. 'Now, all previous Home Defence exercises have emphasized the smooth transition from peace to war in the event of a nuclear attack. In doing so, we have provided ammunition for the peace campaign.'

'In what way?' asked one of the men from the Home Office.

'Simply because there is no defence against such an attack. We all recognize that fact. Britain will be obliterated should the Russians strike. When the Early Warning sounds, there will be a fearful panic not only by the civilian population, but also by the military, those guardians to whom we have designated the tasks of protecting essential supplies, manning routes, securing vital installations, et cetera.'

'The peace campaign and the survival instinct?' suggested Mary Masitter.

'Exactly,' said Dewhurst. 'The peace campaigners focus on the nuclear aspect and show that it is a threat to our very existence. That is why operation *Brave Defender* has

78

to concern itself with the conventional rather than the nuclear threat.'

'The shift of focus,' said the man from the Home Office.

Dewhurst nodded. 'By having a conventional threat, we will push the peace campaigners out into the cold.'

'And what form will this conventional threat take?' asked Masitter.

'Armed Russian troops on the British mainland,' replied Dewhurst. He watched the looks of dismay and incomprehension among the groups.

'We have received no word about such troops,' said a senior representative from the Defence Ministry.

'You have now,' said Dewhurst. 'An elite body of troops, the *Spetsnaz*, has been infiltrating this country for over five years. They have established themselves in secret, close to vital installations. Their task, in the event of war with Soviet Russia, would be sabotage, murder and mayhem.'

'I take it,' said Masitter, 'that this information has only just come to light?'

'Quite correct. It would be nigh impossible to root them out. So we must prepare our Home Defence troops to deal with them in the likelihood of hostilities. In the run up to *Brave Defender*, as the planning for the operation becomes finalised, several senior officers of my Department will be attached to your Ministries. Their tasks will be to ensure that all information, all public announcements and pronouncements about *Brave Defender* will stress the fact that the greatest danger to the security and well-being of Britain lies not with the nuclear, but with the conventional threat. Posed by the *Spetsnaz*.'

Port Simpson, Canada

I

'Kek-kek-kek.' Nike raised his binoculars. 'Kek-kek-kek,' chattered the Harrier as he focused on the hovering form. Then he lost it. He found it again as it quartered low over the reed-beds, its wings canted upwards. He followed the hawk's flight, saw that it was a male, grey body with black wing tips and a pronounced white rump, then lost it as it crossed the River Skeena, his field of vision interrupted by the firs which surrounded his hide.

He traced the river downstream to Port Rupert, picked out the airport, traversed right to Port Simpson, then adjusted the focus on the Zeiss to fix upon the road that ran eastwards from the port. He spotted the right and left forks, stayed with the main avenue, coming back upon himself, until he saw the track that wound across the flat lands and into the foothills, terminating at a barred fence that marked the boundary of the small ranch.

A thin plume of smoke rose listlessly from the stone stack of the ranch house. The paddocks were empty and the rails dividing them were weather-worn and near to collapse, while the stable-block showed several missing slates and cried out for a lick of paint. The gravel walkways were disappearing under tufts of grass and weeds and pot-holes dotted the tarmac drive. A Buick estate was parked outside the house whose timbered façade reminded Nike of the rough-hewn wooden cabins of the American West.

Nike nibbled a bar of chocolate as he watched from behind the tree line wrapped in his sleeping bag. The man had been up for an hour working in the stables. Nike put down his glasses and rolled over on to his side, closing his eyes. There wasn't a dog on the ranch.

Towards noon, Nike saw the man, suitcase in hand, climb into the Buick and drive off. The car joined the main highway into Port Simpson, but turned off later on to the Port Rupert road. 'He'll be gone for a couple of days,' guessed Nike. 'Time to get ready.' He had already noted the wooden shed at the side of the house that contained the generator.

II

Nike waited in the house for two days until the man returned. He had seen the Buick turn off on to the track and went downstairs and waited. Soon he heard the car bouncing up the driveway. He sat down in the chair facing the front entrance. Dewhurst had complicated matters with his orders but Nike had been up to the task. The car came to a halt. The door was slammed shut. Footsteps climbing the steps. The case dropped to the floor. Keys jangling, lock turning, brass knob moving. Nike threw the switch.

Gallagher roared in agony, a big, heavy man whimpering. Nike turned off the electricity and picked up his knife. He stepped over the cable and opened the door. Gallagher was on his knees, moaning, his right hand weakly grasping the brass door knob. There was a smell of singed hair. Gallagher tried to look up as his arm fell away limply.

Nike lifted Gallagher's head by roughly grabbing a handful of brown hair. He smiled as he slowly cut the man's throat, as ordered, from ear to ear with his stiletto, reminding himself as he did so to let the horses out into the paddock before he left. The poor beasts needed some fresh air.

London, England

The bed was creaking.

'I thought you said you fixed it,' said Julia breathlessly.

'I did,' gasped Maitland. He spoke into the spread of her hair. 'Sounds better, doesn't it?'

She dug her nails into his back.

Maitland kept driving on. He kissed her cheek, her forehead, her lips. She arched her back and wrapped her legs round his. He tried to pull her closer, pressing and grinding his stomach and hips into Julia's pliant flesh. She bit his shoulder, but his moan was lost in the bed noise.

He was coming and he wanted to prolong it. He tried to make his mind blank; he closed his eyes, but it didn't work. He was losing control. Julia began to squirm and writhe beneath him. Two hundred and sixty one times seven, he thought, and he laid out the calculation in his mind, white figures against a black background. The answer materialized. He produced another, this time much longer, but it was so complicated he lost the thread. Julia's fingernails caressed his scrotum, and release was immediate.

Their bodies were locked together, separated only by a film of perspiration. Her fringe was plastered to her forehead, and he could feel a run of sweat all along his spine. They kissed and rocked back and forth on the bed.

'That was nice,' she murmured.

'Good,' he said. He propped himself up on one elbow. 'I'm sorry,' he added.

'What for?' She opened her eyes wide.

He stroked her cheek. 'You know.'

'You're overworked, Ollie. That's all.'

They had been arguing frequently of late. Maitland knew he was to blame. It wasn't overwork; it was the work itself that troubled him. He trusted her, but he couldn't confide in her fully. He had to talk to her in an oblique, roundabout way about his work, and became angry with her when she could not understand what he was getting at. Paradoxically, he doubted whether he could have completed his tasks without Julia's support. Her very presence at his side was all that he needed. He was frustrated; he needed a sounding board to help him sort out what he felt about what he was doing. Perhaps if they were married . . .

But deep down Maitland feared that if he ever did confide in her, she would not approve of what he was doing. In many ways, she reminded him of his mother. Not physically, but there was a great similarity in their kind and caring natures. The two women had met and had immediately taken to each other. Maitland believed his work was driving a wedge between himself and Julia, forcing them apart. If he allowed it to continue, he believed it would also affect his relationship with his mother. She had already been sacrificed once on the altar of his father's ambition. Maitland did not want it to happen again.

The telephone rang. Maitland answered, pulling their bodies apart as he did so.

'Simon,' he said brightly into the receiver. He listened to what his uncle had to say. His arms began to shake; he sensed the colour draining from his face. His breath came in short gasps.

'Ollie, Ollie,' cried Julia. She shook his shoulder. 'What's wrong? What's the matter?'

Witney, England

I

Simon had interposed himself between Maitland and his father.

'Amen,' finished the vicar. He blessed the coffin. Maitland stepped forward and threw a handful of earth on his mother's coffin. It made a dull sound as it landed and scattered across the lid. The grave-diggers wrestled with the ropes, mindful of their feet among the array of bright flowers and sombre wreaths. The rest of the mourners made their contribution as the coffin was lowered to its final resting place. Maitland's father cast a red rose.

Maitland, Julia and Simon stood to one side and watched as the spades went to work. His father was in the crowd, shaking hands, receiving commiserations, occasionally smiling, playing the sorrowful widower. Maitland was filled with disgust.

II

Thompson was dispensing drinks to the mourners in the drawing room. Maitland was hemmed in by the vicar and two ladies from the village. He wanted to speak to his father who was nowhere to be seen.

'I will try, Mrs Willoughby,' he said to the taller of the two women. 'But my work keeps me in London.'

'We understand, Oliver. Perhaps you could bring a few friends,' she suggested.

'That would be nice,' said the vicar. 'Some new faces in the church wouldn't go amiss.'

Maitland agreed to come to the fund-raising dinner. He caught Simon's attention who came to the rescue. Maitland extricated himself with a promise of a donation to the roof fund, and went in search of his father.

The study. He opened the door without knocking.

'. . . squeezed between the peace campaigners and the Russian drive for disarmament talks . . .'

Maitland recognized the man who was talking. Sir James Fitch-Heyes, an old friend and business colleague of his father's, chairman of Airwork Industries, which supplied both the Ministry of Defence and the Pentagon with weaponry. The man standing next to his father he did not know.

'Oliver,' said his father in a voice laced with warning.

Maitland shook hands with Sir James.

Professor Irving Bernhardt introduced himself. 'Glad to know you, Oliver.'

Maitland's father came to stand in front of Oliver. 'What do you want, Oliver?'

'This is your wife's funeral. And you turn it into a business meeting,' said Maitland scornfully.

'Don't you dare speak to me like that,' he hissed.

'You cannot even give her a day of your time. Your performance at the graveside was admirable for its brevity and total lack of compassion. It was all that was required of you for public consumption, wasn't it?'

He tried to edge Maitland backwards through the open door, while at the same time glancing over his shoulder to see the effect his son's outburst was having on his two friends.

'Get out,' he spat. 'Get out. Don't you ever . . .'

Maitland stood his ground. A realization had come over him that morning. Mother had gone; father had lost his weapon. No longer could he plague and torment her with the shortcomings of her son, exploiting her loving nature, knowing that he, Maitland, would always acquiesce to his father's demands rather than see her hurt.

He had prayed at his mother's graveside for the courage to confront his father. Something brushed his arm, it was Julia. She stood by his side and clasped his hand. 'No. You get out. Get out of my house.'

Maitland was free at last.

Chamar Pass, Afghanistan

He was still Hasham. Had been ever since that fateful night at the Presidential Palace. He had not heard his true name, Alexei Tabelov, used again. As soon as the KGB Commandos had realized that they had slain their own leader, Colonel Bayerenov, they had hurriedly retreated with the body, leaving Hasham for dead. When the Afghanistanis loyal to the dead President had returned to the scene of carnage, they had found Hasham badly wounded in the Great Hall. They had carried him off, and had hidden him from the Russians in Kabul for more than a year until he was fully recovered. He was a hero to them, a man who had tried to defend his President against the evil Russian horde.

Later, he had been taken into the mountains of Nuristan, Land of Light, and had joined up with a band of *Mujahideen* rebels. But not before he had managed to contact the Embassy to report that he was still alive. He had even managed a meeting with Colonel Vytutin, Bayerenov's replacement, and had fixed up some basic means for continuing communication. Now, after more than two years in the mountains killing his fellow Russians and their Afghanistani allies, he wanted to get back to Kabul. To Russia. To Azerbaydzhan, the place of his birth. He longed for the mountains of his homeland. He yearned for a bowl of *dovta*, sour milk and meat soup, his favourite, which his mother had cooked for him in his youth.

Instead, he would have to do with the meagre fare

Massoud Shah had just distributed to the group, dried mulberries and a chunk of hard, unleavened bread.

Hasham sat with his back to a rock, the goathair blanket hanging loosely around his shoulders, while he nibbled the hard bread with the patience and fortitude of an anchorite. The sun was rising and soon it would be time to sleep.

They were moving down into the Panjshir Valley for the summer fighting season after a long rest and recuperation period in Pakistan. Their arsenal had been greatly increased thanks to the Americans, and now, besides the erratic and untrusty SAM-7 missile launchers, they had supplemented their fire power with two .50 calibre Browning machine guns capable of bringing down a helicopter at a range of four miles. Massoud Shah was overjoyed with them. They gave him enormous prestige, not only amongst his own men, but also amongst the other rival bands of *Mujahideen*.

He tried to sleep, but could not find a comfortable position. His right side ached, a legacy of the slaughter in Kabul. But he was fatigued, too. His whole body throbbed with the pain of muscular exhaustion. The night before they had crossed the highest point of the Pass. On the northern face, the snow had been eroded into frozen pillars, two feet high, and about a foot apart, what mountaineers called *névés pénitents*, and traversing the face had been laborious and strenuous. Mohamed Jan had broken his ankle and would have to be carried down to the Valley.

The Panjshir Valley. He knew that the average Russian trooper held the place in fearful dread. He had seen it in the way they approached their intermittent incursions into the *Mujahideen* stronghold. The Russian commanders had no control over their men, especially when Massoud Shah's men opened fire on them from expertly concealed ambushes. It was always a rout, the Russians would turn tail and run. Those that couldn't, the wounded and the dying, usually perished screaming at the hands of the *Mujahideen* and their childishly sadistic games, their bodies the objects of nightmarish stories when later recovered by the helicopter crews.

Hasham always made sure that he killed his Russian brothers cleanly. He had to kill to survive without suspicion within the *Mujahideen*. He salved his conscience with the thought that he did inflict some damage on the rebels with the information he periodically supplied to Kabul. But it wasn't enough. The *Mujahideen*, bands of illiterate, ragged, half-starving fighters, were holding at bay one hundred thousand well-armed and superbly equipped Soviet troops. The same troops that Western politicians warned their people would one day sweep across the European plain to engulf and enslave the NATO allies. He smiled wanly to himself.

And these *Mujahideen* were of the same breed as the Islamic Fundamentalists who fought the West in Iran and Lebanon. But in Afghanistan, the West gave them their support simply because they were killing Russians. If the KGB had only handled the death of President Amin with patience and tact, then Mother Russia would not be embroiled in this present quagmire, he thought.

Massoud Shah approached and knelt before him. He was dressed as all the group were, baggy trousers, dark homespun coat, and floppy Chitrali hat, held in place by a red scarf tied underneath the chin. He wore no insignia of rank or anything else to distinguish him as leader of the most successful legion in the area. In a way, Hasham admired the man, his strength, his courage, his determination to oust the Russians and return Afghanistan to the archaic peasant ways it had enjoyed for centuries. As he spoke, Hasham could not help but feel a twinge of regret for the man who was about to lead his men into a Soviet trap on the banks of the River Panjshir.

London, England

I

She had to shout above the blare of the disco music. 'What's wrong darling?'

'Nothing.' Maitland tried to make his voice casual as he leant closer.

'You look as if you've just seen a ghost.'

He took hold of her hand. 'Why don't we go? Have an early night? I don't think I can take the noise any longer.'

'You don't look as if you could take an early night either.' Her tongue glided across her shining lips, and she arched her eyebrows.

He winked at her. 'Want to bet? Do me a favour, old girl. Call a taxi. Your place.' He nudged her elbow.

As she began to push her way across the crowded dance floor, a man in his mid-forties took her place on the bench seat. He pressed his shoulder hard against Maitland's.

'What the hell are you doing back, Jimmy-Jack?'

'I like London, Mr Oliver.' He held a glass of beer in one hand.

'And discos?'

Jimmy-Jack shrugged his shoulders. 'Can't stay buried forever.'

'If you want to stay alive you do.'

Deep lines of sadness crossed the man's face. 'Yes. I suppose so. But then you sit alone in your safe house. Like a monk. And you get to thinking. Lonely in that house you know.' He paused. 'Nice place, too. I have you to thank for that, Mr Oliver.'

'Is that why you came all this way? To thank me?'

'And you've a steady income every month. But you can't go out and spend it. Scared to. And you know one day they will find you. They'll come and put that black bag over your head, kneel you down. Then blow your brains out. Yes, they will. A merciful release I used to tell myself.'

'I'll see you, Jimmy-Jack.' Maitland got half-way out of his seat, but the man's restraining arm held him back.

'Sit and talk a while longer, Mr Oliver. At least until the young lady comes back. It's not very often I get to talk to people.' He knocked back his drink in one gulp. 'So, I got to thinking. If they're going to get me one day, why not have a good time in between. Better than sitting miserably at home waiting for them to call.'

'You didn't like Canada I take it?'

'A fine place. But a long way from my roots. Noxy Gallagher thought so too.'

'Who?' Maitland's voice rose several decibels.

'Don't tell me you've forgotten Gallagher?'

'Never,' growled Maitland.

'I thought not. Just surprised that I'd seen him, eh?'

'And lived to talk about it.'

Jimmy-Jack chuckled. 'A fine figure of a man was Noxy.'

'Thug. Cold-blooded murderer would be a better description.'

'He had his dark side, I'll admit that. But a good man all the same. A bugger for the horses, you know?'

'Where did you see him, Jimmy-Jack?'

'The first time?'

Maitland looked at Jimmy-Jack. The man was smiling,

showing his teeth, crooked moss-covered tombstones. He decided Jimmy-Jack was playing a game with him. Before he could reply, he saw Julia out of the corner of his eye. He held up a hand and spread his fingers. 'Five minutes,' he mouthed at her. He saw her hesitate, smile, then disappear among the swirling bodies and flailing limbs on the dance floor.

'A place called Etobicoke. That's in Ontario.'

'When?'

'Some time ago now. Etobicoke is where the Woodbine racecourse is. A handy little place. Fifteen miles from Toronto, and only two miles from the airport. So, you fly in. Have some fun with the horses. Then straight back home.' Jimmy-Jack laughed and shook his head.

'What's so funny?'

'Well it was a laugh the first time we met. We bumped into each other at the Pay Window.'

'I can't see how you find it funny. Not a man in your position.'

'Ah. You don't know the half of it, Mr Oliver. We saw each other, then both turned and ran. We met up twenty minutes later at the airport, both of us scrambling to get on the first available plane out of there.' Jimmy-Jack slapped his knees in delight.

Maitland was confused. He narrowed his eyes. 'What are you saying, Jimmy-Jack?'

'Don't you see? I thought he had come to get me. And . . .'

'And Gallagher thought you'd come to get him,' said Maitland slowly.

'Right. We both twigged at the same time. What a laugh. We sank some drink that night. And the next day.'

'I don't believe you, Jimmy-Jack.'

'That Noxy Gallagher was out in Canada on an MI5

pension just like myself? And why ever not? You couldn't possibly know everything that went on.'

'Not that bastard. We would never have had any dealings with that killer.'

'Now that's where you're wrong, Mr Oliver. He worked for MI5 for nigh on three years. Not as long as myself, I'll say. But deserving of his pension all the same.'

'That's what he told you, did he? When you first met?' Maitland laughed.

'No. Not at first. But we saw a lot of each other after that. I don't see why you're so sceptical about Noxy. How many people knew I worked for you? How many of your own people had their own man inside the movement and eventually arranged a safe pension for them? Tell me.'

'Where is he now?'

'He was living outside a town called Port Simpson in British Columbia. I went there a few times. Had a small stud farm. Bred some horses. Not the racing variety. And like me, he missed the old country.'

'Especially after a couple of drinks.'

'True. And we talked a lot, of course. And then last winter I came down with a bout of pneumonia. Was laid up for three months. I didn't hear from Noxy. So when I was better, I went across to see him. His farm was very isolated. He rarely had a visitor.' Jimmy-Jack leant forward and picked up Maitland's drink. 'Don't mind?'

'Help yourself.'

'Thanks.' He sipped it slowly. 'When I got there, Noxy was dead. He'd been dead for at least a week. That's what I guessed. The horses were all loose in their paddocks. And Noxy's body. Well the smell and . . .'

'Spare me the details, Jimmy-Jack.' Maitland finished off Julia's gin and tonic.

'Throat cut. Almost decapitated.' He rubbed his chin thoughtfully. 'So, here I am.'

'You feel it's safer here than in Canada.'

'Depends who's chasing you, doesn't it? No. I've brought you something from Noxy.' He pulled out a buff envelope from his inside pocket. 'Noxy asked me to give it to you personally. In the event of . . .'

'What is it? And why me? I didn't know the man. And there's nothing I want to know about that bastard. He got what he deserved.' He wouldn't take the envelope.

'As I said, we used to talk a lot,' said Jimmy-Jack. 'About the old days mainly. I told him about you. He seemed to like you. That's why he wanted you to have this.' He pushed the envelope into Maitland's hand.

'What's in it?'

'I don't know the fine details. Just the general outline.'

'I'll take it then,' said Maitland reluctantly. 'I don't work the Irish desk any more. But I'll pass it on.'

'You don't see it, do you Mr Oliver?'

'See what?'

'Noxy had his throat cut. That wasn't an IRA execution. They'd have shot him cleanly in the head. No, my boy. Noxy's death was MI5 taking its revenge. Noxy knew too much.'

II

Julia had gone home alone in the taxi. She had understood. Maitland had felt hungry. He hadn't eaten earlier and his stomach growled at him, as had Julia when she had found out. She had admonished him again for too much drinking and he had promised her to cut down.

Since his mother's death, he had to admit that he had

been drinking more and more. It was a combination of things, he supposed; the final break with his father and the work with Gouzenko, which thank God was coming to an end. The book had been published and distributed and it had been well publicised. The film had just been completed and would be shown shortly on television. There were very few people in Britain, and the West for that matter, who had not heard of the *Spetsnaz* and the threat they posed. He had done a good job. Sir Robert MacKenzie, the Director, had warmly congratulated him. And so had Dewhurst.

He smiled to himself; perhaps that was why he had been drinking so much. A compliment from Dewhurst was not something he would want to boast about.

It worried him that Dewhurst liked what he had done, for it was something that Maitland was not proud of. Now, it was almost over, he thought, and he would be able to spend more time with Julia and reduce his dependence on the demon drink.

'There's an Indian nearby,' said Jimmy-Jack.

'That'll do,' said Maitland. 'I fancy a curry.'

III

They were the only customers in the restaurant, outnumbered two to one by the yawning waiters. They sat with their backs to the wall which was covered by a red, patterned paper that had a thicker pile than the curry-stained carpet with its well-trodden gulleys running between tables, toilet and door. The lighting was by Wurlitzer, bright neon strips that hummed a despondent accompaniment to the off-key twang of the sitar muzak.

The waiter brought the beer they had asked for as they

had entered, and Maitland ordered a *Jingha Malaicurry* for himself. 'Do you want anything?' he asked Jimmy-Jack.

The Irishman had his head submerged in his pint. 'No thanks,' he replied. 'I never eat on an empty stomach.'

'What made you turn informer, Jimmy-Jack?' asked Maitland suddenly as the waiter retreated to the steaming kitchen. He hadn't come to terms with his own attitude towards men such as Jimmy-Jack and the whole question of loyalty to a cause, to a country. When he had left Ireland for London, he hadn't given the problem a second thought; but the man's sudden reappearance had rekindled the ambiguous feeling he had always had. That and the work he was currently doing for Dewhurst.

'Eh?' spluttered Jimmy-Jack, his face reddening. 'Informer is it? Not me.'

'Well what are you, then? What would you call yourself?'

'A Republican. Born and bred.'

'The men you betrayed would have another name for you.'

'Republicans are fighting for a united Ireland. They don't recognize the border or the Dublin government. They are our enemies. As the British are. But only the politicians and the soldiers. Not innocent women and children who are put in the firing line as primary targets.'

'You didn't believe in the tactics of the High Command?'

Jimmy-Jack nodded his head. 'Indiscriminate bombings, sectarian killing. These were never part of the Republican's fight. But if the boys at the top think those are the tactics to employ, then men like me have to go along. You can't resign from the IRA.'

The waiter ambled up to the table with Maitland's meal and two more beers.

Jimmy-Jack continued. 'I still believe in the cause as such. But not the cause above everything, not above the murder of innocents. The men you caught on information I gave were out and out killers. They were only interested in the killing. The cause meant nothing to them.'

'I understand,' said Maitland slowly. 'Is that another of the reasons why you came back with Gallagher's letter?'

'I suppose so, Mr Oliver,' replied the Irishman. 'Tell me, Mr Oliver, would you put your country above everything? Right or wrong?'

'I don't know, Jimmy-Jack.'

'Perhaps the letter will help you decide.'

IV

There were tears in Maitland's eyes. He screwed up Gallagher's letter into a ball and threw it against the wall. He kicked out at it. 'Lies. All lies,' he sobbed. 'Bastard Gallagher.'

It was close to dawn. He hadn't drawn the curtains. The black of night had been overtaken by an insipid grey. It had taken him a couple of hours to read and fully understand the contents of the letter because he had been drinking as he did so. He had started his task as an atheist, shifted to agnosticism, and had then been converted to the state of belief. Because he did remember. The memory had catapulted itself into his thoughts and leapt up to demand attention.

He remembered. His mother telling him of President Kennedy. And he remembered a trip to Paris and how it had terminated at Heathrow at the same time that a flight from Copenhagen had landed. He remembered.

Moscow, Russia

Feliks Edmundovich Dzerzhinsky, a Pole of aristocratic origins, emerged from Butyrki gaol in 1917 to set up the All Russia Extraordinary Commission for Combatting Counter-Revolution, Speculation, Sabotage and Misconduct in Office, on the express orders of Lenin. This Committee, known under its acronym *Vecheka*, later shortened to *Cheka*, became synonymous with terror, murder and suppression, and was the direct antecedent of the *Komitet Gosudarstvennoy Bezopasnosti*, the notorious KGB.

A goatee-bearded statue of the grandfather of Soviet terror, unveiled by Nikita Kruschev in 1961, commands the centre of Dzerzhinsky Square under the long shadow of the Kremlin. Facing the statue is an ornate, ochre-coloured building of six storeys which, until the Revolution, housed the offices of the All Russian Company. After World War II, German prisoners and slave labourers were conscripted to erect a ten-storey, Stalinesque extension. These two buildings, behind which stands the infamous Lubyanka prison, are the headquarters of the KGB, Moscow Centre.

Like his predecessors, General Mikhailovich Chebrikov, the current Chairman of the KGB, has a suite of offices on the sixth floor of the original building which overlooks the Square and the statue. On the first Monday in July, the Chairman stood at one of the windows staring unseeingly in the direction of the Kremlin while listening distractedly to Colonel Konstantin of the Technical Support Directorate.

'The two amplifiers of the dual-trace oscilloscope receive the waveforms of the two sound tracks. On the screen, using two separate time bases, the cathode-ray beams pick out the frequency differences and similarities which are photographed immediately.' Konstantin picked up the sheaf of photographs. 'We use the *Polaroid Land* stock for the photoprints which has an *ASA* equivalent of ten thousand.' He coughed to say that he had finished.

It was a few minutes before Chebrikov replied. 'And you have a match?'

'Yes, Comrade,' said Konstantin. 'It was as you suspected. Captain Oleg Davidovich Gouzenko of the GRU. Defected to the West in Amsterdam in November 1981.'

There was a knock at the door which opened almost immediately. 'They are ready for you, Comrade Chairman.'

'Thank you, Vadim,' said Chebrikov to his adjutant. Vadim held the door open as Chebrikov passed through accompanied by Konstantin, then skipped on ahead to lead the two men down the hallway to the Chairman's private cinema.

Marshal Ustinov, Defence Minister, sat on the back row. In front of him, spread across the centre row, were three generals. Chebrikov made it four. He took a seat at the front, while Konstantin and Vadim stood to one side. Chebrikov pressed a series of buttons on his console, and his audience settled in to watch a video recording of a film which had been shown two nights previously on British television.

He had spent most of the day viewing the recording with Konstantin and his band of technicians, and so he

102

allowed himself a short catnap as the others took their turn. He would have to be very careful how he began the proceedings: he did not want General Yevgeni Lyalin from the rival GRU storming out in a pique and starting trouble behind his back. He had enough problems with the disaster of *Golden Fleece* and the failure to unmask *Cedar* without the worry of the Gouzenko affair blowing up in his face, but Ustinov was on his side.

The giant video screen suddenly lost its colour to be replaced by a whistling black and white storm of static. Chebrikov opened his eyes and jabbed at the console: the overhead lights blinked into life, the screen went blank, and the shutters rolled open, to admit the last traces of daylight. He stood and faced the assembled group.

'They have a saying in the West: you've read the book, now you've seen the film.' The expressionless faces that stared back at him said he had been wrong to attempt a light-hearted approach. 'Or something like that,' he added lamely.

Chebrikov stepped nearer to his guests, gathering his thoughts. 'It is a year ago that the *Spetsnaz* came to our attention. A book was published in Britain, written by a traitor. He used the name Major Illya Serbsky, and claimed to be a former member of our armed forces. You all received a copy of this piece of British disinformation, and you will remember most of the salient points which the traitor reiterated on the film.'

'Do you know what is behind the British ploy?' asked Ustinov.

'A simple propaganda exercise. The British, urged on by the Americans, have to convince their people that there is a real and tangible threat on their doorstep, an enemy lurking in the shadows and the hedgerows, waiting to strike. The *Spetsnaz* is supposed to be thirty-thousand strong, men and women trained to Olympic athlete standards, all fully conversant with the latest intelligence techniques of infiltration, sabotage and assassination.' Chebrikov paused. 'With the *Spetsnaz* supposedly already operating inside Britain, the government will be able to whip up sufficient anti-Soviet hysteria at home and throughout the NATO bloc, so that the deployment of Trident, Cruise, Pershing and research into Star Wars will pass without question or protest.'

Ustinov intervened on cue. 'So the invention of the *Spetsnaz* is a part of the West's overall strategy of increasing the pace for the arms race while maintaining its position that recent deployments are simply in response to our belligerence?'

'That is the way I see it, Marshal,' replied Chebrikov.

'Who is this Major Serbsky? Have you been able to identify him?' asked Army Chief, Boris Soldatov.

'We have had our suspicions ever since the book was published. Ten possibles. In the film, Serbsky was blacked out, but his voice, in Russian and English, was clearly heard. Computer enhancement techniques could not give a recognizable face. But we were more fortunate with the voice print,' said Chebrikov as he paced backwards and forwards.

'I take it the traitor is not one of your wayward sons?' asked Lyalin with a sneer.

'Comrade General, I do not think it matters from what arm of the services the defector originated. What matters is what he has said and what use the British are making of it.' Lyalin nodded and sat back relaxed. Chebrikov was pleased. 'The defector is one Captain Oleg Gouzenko.' Chebrikov saw Lyalin bristle. He continued quickly. 'He is making use of a top secret proposal that was submitted to the Politburo in 1962 by a predecessor of mine, Vladimir Semichastny Vadim.' He nodded to his adjutant.

Vadim distributed four buff folders to the group. Chebrikov noted that Lyalin did not enquire about how he had obtained the original voice print of Gouzenko.

'The American blockade of Cuba was in effect at the time,' said Chebrikov. 'International tension was high. Semichastny's report called for the organization and training of an elite force of troops whose task would be to infiltrate the Western democracies to prepare the ground for our own troops should negotiations fail and war became inevitable. Semichastny called his troops *Spetsnaz*.'

'Semichastny's report was never acted upon by the Politburo,' said Ustinov.

'No,' replied Chebrikov. 'Semichastny disgraced himself, and greatly embarrassed the Kremlin, in his attempt to suborn the Yale Professor, Baaghoorn, the following year. Comrade Andropov, who took his place, did not press the matter of the *Spetsnaz* any further with the Politburo.' Lyalin was nodding slowly as Chebrikov spoke. Chebrikov felt confident that with his admission of past KGB failings, he would have Lyalin's cooperation from now on, despite the man's knowledge that one of his underlings in the GRU was responsible for the present problem.

Ustinov was leafing through his folder. 'The reason for this, er, discussion, Comrade General?' he asked casually.

Chebrikov nodded. 'The West now believe in the *Spetsnaz*. In three weeks' time, the British will hold their largest Home Defence exercise since the last war, *Brave Defender*. The *Spetsnaz* will be the enemy within. Thousands of troops will be mobilized to deal with these infiltrators who, as we know, do not exist. Yet.' He stood beneath the video screen. 'The Premier asked for this meeting. It is his wish that we give the British what they say already exists. The *Spetsnaz*. And your total cooperation, Comrades, is called for. We will recruit and train from all sections of the armed forces a *Spetsnaz* force that must be operational in eighteen months. It will be thirty-thousand strong, men and women . . .'

Troon, Scotland

I

In his more forthright moods, Sir Robert MacKenzie would claim a close, common ancestry with Sir George MacKenzie of Rosehaugh, *Bloody MacKenzie*, Lord Advocate of Scotland in the seventeenth century, to whom the gallows was the only cure for all the ills that beset his beloved country.

However, in a lighter vein, Sir Robert was disposed to boast of a kinsman of a much later period, a banker from Barassie, who together with a group of notables from Glasgow, Kilmarnock and Prestwick, founded the Troon Golf Club in 1878. The Director-General of MI5 was a life member of Royal Troon.

Maitland had booked a room at the Sun Court Hotel, and had taken a taxi to Sir Robert's summer home which overlooked the eighteenth green and the clubhouse.

He was shown into the drawing room by a young housemaid, and Lady Gavine MacKenzie, dressed in a tailored tweed suit, gave him the briefest of courtesies by informing him that her husband was on the links and that the gardener would show him the way to the clubhouse. She patently did not approve of subordinates interrupting the holidays of their superiors.

The Club Secretary was on hand to greet Maitland as he arrived, forewarned by the formidable Lady MacKenzie, and he was shown into the Smoke Room to await Sir

Robert's return. Maitland insisted upon keeping his attaché case with him, much to the chagrin of the officious Secretary.

Maitland idled away an hour, reading the Captains roll, examining a display of golf clubs almost two hundred years old, and trying to discover why individual holes on the course had such peculiar names as *Tel-el-Kebir*, *The Monk* and *Burmah*.

He struck up a conversation with a florid-faced man who sported spats and explained how the various names arose. 'The third is called *Gyaws*,' he said, in his distinctive English accent. 'A gyaws being a hollow or channel with a spring flowing through it. In fact the spring, or burn as they say up here, runs across the third and sixteenth fairways.'

Maitland was impressed. His education, however, was interrupted by the arrival of Sir Robert.

II

Maitland was returned to the drawing room, while Sir Robert went to shower and change. He was allowed a pot of coffee, but he supplemented it with several liberal helpings of his host's malt whisky in order to quell the nervous tension in his stomach.

When Sir Robert eventually put in an appearance, dressed in grey slacks and a light blue sweater, his dark hair was still damp and shiny. MacKenzie had the physique of a clothes-horse, narrow and angular. He didn't dress; rather his clothing was draped over his spindly frame which gave the impression of a well-heeled scarecrow.

Maitland handed over his dossier without explanation, inviting the Director-General to read it before commenting either on his unscheduled arrival or on the contents of the file. While he read, Maitland fretted and made further inroads into the Glenmorangie much to the annoyance of MacKenzie.

When Sir Robert had finished, he gathered the papers into their correct order and put them to one side as if they were somehow unclean, wrinkling his nose as he did so. He rubbed his hands together in a washing motion and sat back in his armchair. He crossed his right leg over his left, then curled the right foot behind and below the left calf, as if winding himself up for the start of his part of the session.

'Why have you brought this to me?' he asked. 'After all, Alan Dewhurst is directly responsible to me.'

Maitland had taken a gamble. Gallagher's letter which had detailed the planning and execution of the assassination at Mullaghmore showed that only Burton and Dewhurst had been involved. That did not mean that Sir Robert had been unaware of what Dewhurst had been up to, but Maitland believed that Dewhurst had acted without his superior's sanction.

However, should it turn out that MacKenzie had approved the deed, then he, Maitland, had sufficient ammunition to force the Director to bring it out into the open. 'You believe what's written there?' asked Maitland cautiously.

'That's not up to me to decide,' said MacKenzie. He picked up Gallagher's letter from the file. 'This could be a piece of Soviet disinformation. Had you thought of that?'

'Yes, I had. But the dates, the times, the places. They all coincide with my own findings about Burton and Dewhurst,' said Maitland.

'And Burton is dead.' MacKenzie waved the letter at Maitland. 'This, like all the other documents, is a photocopy.'

'I have the original letter.'

'I see,' said MacKenzie thoughtfully. 'You don't trust me. You think I am involved.'

'I have to . . .'

'That's quite all right, Oliver. I understand. And I can assure you that I knew absolutely nothing whatsoever of this, er, operation.'

'Thank you, sir,' replied Maitland. He relaxed a little. 'When charges are brought against Dewhurst I will make all the originals available.'

'Charges?' exploded MacKenzie. 'Charges? Are you mad?'

'No, er. I don't understand,' stammered Maitland, stunned by the outburst.

MacKenzie wagged a finger at Maitland. 'Let me tell you, young man. If there is any substance in what you have given me, then Dewhurst will be removed from the Service. But there will be no charges. And certainly no courts, no trial, which is what I imagine you envisage.'

'But this is murder,' protested Maitland.

'You've appointed yourself judge and jury?' sneered MacKenzie. 'How dare you? The case against Dewhurst will be decided on its merits by a duly appointed commission which will look at all the evidence.'

'Yes, yes. Of course,' said Maitland.

'But it will be an internal affair. We can't afford to let something like this get out into the public domain. Think of what it would do to the Service. MI5 would be crucified. The government would be brought down. And without a credible, viable Security Service to guard the nation's interests, the Soviets would be all over us. Had you thought of that?'

'Perhaps not as fully as I should have.'

'And this coming at a time when we are embroiled in the miners' strike which is destroying the entire social fabric of the country. Can you imagine what the miners' leader would make of it?' MacKenzie uncrossed his legs and stretched them out in front of him. 'And then there is your own predicament.'

'What predicament?' asked Maitland.

'In compiling your dossier, you made copies from MI5's files and sources. Unauthorised copies. You removed them from Curzon Street. You have broken your oath of loyalty to the Service. You are in breach of the Official Secrets Act. I presume you have secreted the original letter and the copies of your research somewhere safe?'

'Yes. I've made four copies of the evidence. They are well hidden.' Maitland was lying. He had only two copies; one was with his uncle Simon, the other was in a bank vault in New York, together with instructions that it was to be made available to the newspapers in the event of his untimely death. 'I admit I have done wrong. But it is a minor infringement compared with what Dewhurst has done.'

'The lesser of two evils is still an evil,' pronounced MacKenzie.

Maitland was confused. He couldn't think straight. He was having to defend himself where he should be attacking Dewhurst.

'I will personally set up an in-house investigation into the allegations,' added MacKenzie. 'If Dewhurst is found guilty, he will be removed. Quietly and without fuss.'

'I appreciate what you have said but . . .'

'But me no buts, Oliver. This is not for public consumption. We are already under the microscope with the threat of a former officer of MI5 to publish his memoirs about the Service. Can you imagine that? Memoirs?' MacKenzie shook his head slowly.

'I understand,' said Maitland.

'Then leave it to me Oliver. I will see that justice is done. If the case is proven, Dewhurst will go.'

London, England

I

The London Office of the British-Bulgarian Trade Union Mission is a flat above a supermarket in Crickland Avenue, just off Streatham Hill. Lawrence Dingle, the Mission's secretary, a short, balding man in his late fifties, is a regular visitor both to the Bulgarian Embassy in Queen's Gate, and that country's capital, Sofia, where he maintains a small villa and a large bank account.

Radoslav Tsanchev, the second most senior Bulgarian diplomat in London, is a frequent caller at the Mission, and details of his dealings with Dingle are monitored by a team from MI5's Surveillance Centre at Grove Park, Camberwell. To date, MI5 have not uncovered anything untoward or suspicious in the activities at the Mission, Dingle and Tsanchev confining their meetings to the work of promoting the international trade union movement. MI5 has Tsanchev listed as the senior member, in Britain, of *Darjavna Sigurnost*, Bulgaria's Secret Service, possibly with the rank of Colonel.

On Friday, June the twenty-first, Dingle was summoned to the Bulgarian Embassy by telephone. He was seen entering and leaving the building, and the times were noted. For the two and a half hours he spent inside the Embassy, there is no record of what transpired. But from that day, Dingle's whole pattern of life changed, which placed an added strain on MI5's manpower, resources and finances, as Dingle charged about the country apparently circulating data and information about his Mission to hundreds of trade union branches.

II

'You are not working for me, Lawrence,' said Tsanchev. 'The *neighbours*, the KGB, are running this. And you'll be one of many. So be careful. Very careful.'

Dingle tried to smile but it was more of a grimace. 'And I report directly to you?'

'Correct. If I'm not available, then leave a message. Use *Statesman* as your key word. I'll get in touch somehow.' Tsanchev leaned across his desk and pointed at the first photograph which was attached to several sheets of typescript. 'He's the most important one. Doctor Pavel Pastukhov. They want him badly.' He lifted the wad of paper and handed it over to Dingle. 'And this one. Do you recognize him?' He turned the photograph round so that Dingle could see it.

'Zarev,' said Dingle. He looked perplexed.

'Yes. He's the next in line. You'll have no trouble spotting him if he's still alive, will you? Not after the time you two spent together.'

'No. I suppose not.'

'Right. First of all read about the events at Godalming and Worplesdon last month, the *Alpha Red Alert*, the SAS mobilization, et cetera. Then study the four files. I want to know if anybody survived the night, and if so, who.'

'And where they are being held?' suggested Dingle.

'Use your contacts in the press and the union branches. Anybody. But find me some answers. A lot depends on this. And Lawrence.' Dingle glanced up and winced as he saw the set of Tsanchev's features. 'No names. No reasons. No mistakes.'

III

Maitland was amused. He stood and went across to the side-table and refilled his cup. Nobody paid any attention to him, so engrossed were the two sides in this latest bout of recrimination and denunciation that periodically afflicted the two Services.

Capstick thumped the table and pointed an accusing finger at the Director of MI6. 'We should have kept you informed?' he shouted, his face crimson. MacKenzie, seated next to him, laid a restraining hand on his shoulder which was ignored. 'And what about MI6 keeping us informed, eh?'

Fordyce shrank in his seat at the ferocity of the attack. 'If you will give me a moment,' he said weakly. The Director of MI6, barely a year into his appointment, sounded harassed. He turned for support to his deputy, Markfield, who was methodically scraping out his pipe bowl with a slim Swiss Army knife, assiduously avoiding eye contact with his superior. Fordyce sighed resignedly.

'Well?' prompted Capstick after an exchange of glances with Dewhurst. To Maitland, who had accompanied the MI5 delegation on Dewhurst's insistence, Capstick had been elected to the role of harrying Fordyce by playing the injured party. The tactic, Maitland assumed, was designed to wrest as much information and as many concessions as possible from Fordyce who had a reputation for vacillation and vacuity.

'Yes,' said Fordyce, biting the bullet. 'Almost a year ago, my former Deputy, Alex Cameron, implemented a top secret operation to throw the Soviet hierarchy into confusion, panic and indecision. Using a serving officer of MI6 whom the Russians had tried to suborn earlier in his career, it was made known to the Kremlin that there was a traitor in the Politburo, codename *Cedar*. Arkady Guk, the KGB resident, was the conduit through which we fed this false notion to the Soviet leadership.'

Maitland resumed his seat. Capstick seemed at a loss for words. MacKenzie saved the day and took up the cudgel. 'It was not my decision to have Guk expelled. The Home Secretary signed the exclusion order without consulting my office.' There was no hint of apology in what he said.

'For goodness sake, he was caught red-handed at a *dubock*,' added Capstick.

'A dead-letter drop,' whispered Markfield to Fordyce when he saw his puzzled frown. Fordyce nodded his understanding.

'The Foreign Office should have been informed,' said Fordyce after a prolonged pause, as if he had been searching for his place in the script.

'And we should have had a *Code Green* from you telling us to leave Guk alone,' countered Capstick quickly.

'That would have made him suspicious,' said Markfield.

'Are you saying we leak?' retorted Capstick.

'Not at all,' replied Markfield. 'But to have withdrawn his surveillance suddenly for the sake of the operation may have alerted him to the fact that something was going on. He may have distrusted our man who was feeding him the information about *Cedar*.'

A momentary truce was declared when Dewhurst called for another round of coffee. Maitland was dispatched to confront the formidable Mrs Engleton with the request. On his return, Capstick was once again in the fray.

'The incidents at Godalming and Worplesdon? That was our bailiwick,' Capstick said, prodding himself in the chest.

'We appreciate that,' said Markfield. Fordyce looked relieved that his Deputy had taken up the challenge. 'But the *Cedar* affair and those two incidents were connected.'

'In what way?' asked Dewhurst.

'The KGB's reaction to the news that there was a traitor inside the Politburo was totally unexpected. Instead of turning the Politburo inside out to find him, they sent over a team of agents to kidnap Alex Cameron in order to extract from him the identity of *Cedar*. Hence Godalming and Worplesdon.'

'I see,' said Capstick. 'We now know why the agents were sent to Britain. But what we want to know is why we were not informed of their presence immediately. We only found out about them after the event, after you had sent in the SAS and eliminated them.'

'It all happened so suddenly and so quickly,' said Fordyce.

'In addition,' said Markfield, 'one of our own people got too close to the whole thing, became emotionally involved. We had to shut up shop pretty smartly.'

'You have seen the Bernhardt Memorandum?' asked Dewhurst.

'Yes,' said Markfield and Fordyce in wary unison, troubled by Dewhurst's interruption.

'And you are aware of Gouzenko's book, and the recent film about the *Spetsnaz*?'

'Yes.' Again in unison.

'And you realize the significance of *Brave Defender* which is currently in operation?' Both men said yes again. 'And it did not occur to you what a tremendous coup it would have been to have captured those Russian agents alive on British soil?' Dewhurst's questioning had, up to that point, been very calm and even. Now he suddenly raised his voice. 'We would have, would we not, then been able to reproduce for the benefit of the British public, physical proof of the existence of the *Spetsnaz*? We could have shown the world and all those bloody peace campaigners that the greatest threat we face is not the bomb, but the *Spetsnaz*.'

Maitland's attention had been wandering. Now he began to take notice. He watched as Fordyce tried to reply, but he was too flustered. Markfield, who had been just about to light his pipe, froze.

'Operation *Brave Defender* would then have been fully justified in the eyes of the population, and the peace campaign would have been on the run. As forecast by Professor Bernhardt,' said Capstick with finality.

'Only one problem,' said Markfield, tapping the table with his pipe. 'The Russian team sent in to kidnap Cameron was made up of four men. And only one of them was a Russian. The other three were mercenaries from the Middle East, Bulgaria . . .'

'Minor details,' said Capstick dismissively.

'The Russian would have been sufficient,' said Dewhurst.

'As I mentioned before, we had to close everything down pretty damn quickly. The Russian incursion and kidnap attempt had to be seen by the Kremlin as a failure so that the myth of *Cedar* remained intact and viable.' Markfield finally lit his pipe. 'The kidnap squad was eliminated.'

'So they are all dead?' asked MacKenzie. 'The Russian and the mercenaries?'

'No,' said Fordyce. Maitland saw the glare that flashed in Markfield's eyes, but Fordyce missed it. He seemed intent on making amends.

'There were survivors?' said Capstick.

'One,' replied Fordyce. 'A man named Todor Zarev.'

IV

Maitland drove them back to Curzon Street. He found it difficult to concentrate driving through the evening rush-hour traffic while trying to keep his attention attuned to what was being said in the back.

'It could only have been Mercer,' said MacKenzie to Dewhurst. 'And Binder was feeding Guk. You were right, Alan, as usual.'

Maitland glanced in the rear-view mirror and saw Dewhurst smile smugly. How he hated the man. He would see MacKenzie later in the week and demand to know how the investigation into Dewhurst's criminality was progressing. Maitland was determined to see the man brought to justice.

Dewhurst began to speak. 'We will do as Fordyce and Markfield asked: when Guk's replacement arrives, surveillance will be kept to a minimum, so that their man can resume contact and continue to prolong the myth of *Cedar*.'

'Agreed,' said MacKenzie. 'And in return . . .?'

'I want the Bulgarian, Zarev,' said Dewhurst. 'We have to have him.'

'Leave that to me, Alan,' said MacKenzie. 'You shall have your man.'

V

It was almost two weeks before Maitland found the time

to re-examine the file on Thomas Todd. Journalist. Deceased. It was there that he had seen Mercer's name mentioned. Now the file had been considerably expanded by several bulky additions from MI5 and MI6 sources.

What struck him first of all was that both Todd and Mercer had been under surveillance at the same time from MI5's Protective Security Branch. The authority had come from the MI6 Director, Fordyce.

Details of the operation involving *Cedar* were now incorporated into Todd's *still life*. At first, Maitland could not see the connection, but as he worked through the reports, he noticed that while Mercer was the Head of Russia Section, he had not been involved in the *Cedar* operation. Except at the very end, during the troubles at Worplesdon. And in the aftermath, Todd and Mercer had died in what he could only conclude were mysterious circumstances.

Mercer, who, if the rumour-mongers were correct, had been at odds with the majority, the *Peterhouse Mafia*, inside MI6. Mercer whom Markfield had said had become *emotionally involved* in the whole *Cedar* affair, a euphemism for interference. Mercer who was now dead. As was Todd.

The initials *NFA* had been appended to the file: *No Further Action*. Maitland wondered whether these initials would one day be his epitaph. For he, too, was *emotionally involved* in his attempt to bring Dewhurst to justice.

VI

'You have to understand, Oliver, that these things take time,' said MacKenzie.

'I appreciate that, sir. But . . .'

'Oliver. The information you supplied me with has been

passed on to a higher authority. They are investigating Mr Dewhurst. I can assure you. But it is a slow process. Every step has to be checked and double-checked. We have to be certain of all our facts. Doubly so because of the nature of the charges you have brought, and the political repercussions that will arise.' He held up his hands to prevent Maitland's interruption. 'And of course, the strictest secrecy has to be observed. It would not do our case any good if we alerted Mr Dewhurst. Or, heaven forbid, the gentlemen of the press.'

'I understand.' Maitland pursed his lips.

'And while all this is going on, MI5 is expected to perform as usual. We have to maintain the appearance of normality. You have to go about your business, as I have to go about mine. Look.' He pointed at the stack of paperwork on his desk. 'I've been inundated with reports about *Brave Defender*. This all came in this morning.' He prodded the stack. 'Preliminary findings indicate that the operation has had no effect whatsoever on people's perception of the bomb.'

'I know. I've seen some of them.'

'There'll be questions. Meetings. Post-mortems. I'll be tied up for days, weeks probably. At the Home Office and the Ministry.'

'Yes,' said Maitland quietly. He had done some checking of his own. Burton's file had been removed from Registry, as had all traces of Dewhurst's movements during the months that preceded the assassination. The links between Burton, Dewhurst and Gallagher no longer existed, except in the dossiers that he had compiled. Had MacKenzie's investigating team removed them? Maitland wanted to believe in that possibility, but there was the lurking suspicion that perhaps it was part of a cover up. He would give the Director a little more time, then he would have to act.

VII

'Mr Maitland is digging his own grave,' said Dewhurst.

'Perhaps,' said MacKenzie. 'But when he's in it, there are the four files which he has placed in safe keeping which will emerge.'

'I have Nike working on that at the moment. And even if they do come to light, nobody will dare publish without consulting us. And we simply slap a ban on the whole episode.'

'I doubt if that would work.'

Dewhurst shrugged. 'Even if all the details are published, we will still be able to handle it. We can always turn it around so that Maitland is implicated. Don't worry, Robert. Everything will turn out as we want it to.'

FINALE

1986

London, England

I

Mike Maguire was tired and dishevelled. It seemed to him as if he had been in constant motion for the past thirty-six hours, and that his feet had lost contact with *terra firma*. Two trans-Atlantic crossings, interrupted by a special briefing from the President's National Security Adviser, and then a mad dash from Heathrow to Curzon Street to update MacKenzie and his team. He yearned for a hot shower and a comfortable bed. Instead he had to make do with a cold room and a rough interrogation.

'It was a natural progression, something the Bernhardt thesis did not take into account,' protested Maguire. 'The White House has been harping on about Libyan sponsorship of international terrorism. People's minds had been successfully focused on Gaddafy as a major threat. But the propaganda had reached saturation point. If it was to continue without some decisive action by the United States being taken, then it would have proved counterproductive. The public would have seen it as propaganda pure and simple.'

'But don't you see,' said Capstick. 'The bombing of Libya was also counter-productive. If Gaddafy is removed . . .'

'He could be dead already,' said Dewhurst.

'Indeed,' said Capstick. 'If he isn't, the chances are he'll be ousted in a coup. But if he goes, so does the focal point of the campaign. Public perception will shift to another enemy.'

'The bomb. Nuclear weapons,' said MacKenzie.

'In fact it has already begun to happen,' said Capstick. 'Ordinary men and women, who wouldn't give a peace campaigner the time of day, are up in arms. You want to see and hear the reaction from those who live close to Mildenhall and Lakenheath.'

'The peace campaigners are rubbing their hands. Recruitment will sky-rocket,' said MacKenzie disgustedly.

'I appreciate all that gentlemen,' said Maguire. 'But the President felt he had been backed up into a corner. He is beginning to waver in his support for Professor Bernhardt's ideas. After all they haven't produced a result yet. It's a no-hitter, according to the White House.'

'This is not some silly American ball game we're engaged in,' retorted MacKenzie.

Maguire looked away, embarrassed by MacKenzie's outburst.

Dewhurst broke the silence. 'It's an ongoing process trying to change the way people think.'

'Look,' said Maguire. 'Operation *Brave Defender* was a failure. Nothing came of that. It turned into a big joke. The peace campaign rolls along, getting bigger every day.'

'We have one or two more irons in the fire that should help,' said Dewhurst.

'The President's running out of time. The Russians are making all the running even with *Cedar* in the Politburo. The Premier has the world media twisted round his little finger. Even the most sceptical are starting to ask why the President hasn't responded to any of the Premier's calls for disarmament talks. America is being seen as the bad guy.'

'The President can always sit down and talk. As long as he remembers not to agree to anything,' said Dewhurst.

Maguire took a few seconds to gather his thoughts. 'The President is determined to keep Star Wars. He won't let that go. It's his baby. The Russians, so the experts say, are prepared to make the most wide-ranging cuts in strategic and long-range weaponry. They might agree to the zero-zero option. But they'll want Star Wars cancelled, and the President will never agree to that. So he's not ready to sit and talk, not prepared to even go through the motions because then the Soviets will come out of any such talks as the angelic peace-makers thwarted by American warmongers.'

II

'Do you have any irons in the fire, Alan?' asked MacKenzie after Maguire had gone.

Dewhurst pondered. 'Yes, Operation *Juniper*.'

'Operation *Juniper*?' said MacKenzie. He closed his eyes as if in thought. 'Operation *Juniper*. Have I been briefed on that? I don't recall having heard it mentioned before.'

'Centred around our friend Todor Zarev.'

'Indeed,' said MacKenzie. 'And when can I expect to see a draft plan of *Juniper*?'

Dewhurst turned his back on his superior. '*Juniper* is already operational,' he said.

'But I . . .' protested MacKenzie.

'I will brief you in due time,' said Dewhurst. He walked over to the door. 'We are running out of time, says Mr Maguire. The Americans have itchy trigger-fingers. Our own government is breathing down our necks demanding results. Operation *Juniper* will give the Prime Minister and the President exactly what they want.'

'That may be so,' protested MacKenzie. 'But I am still Director–General of MI5, Alan. And all operations must go through me for approval.'

'You'll approve it. In due time.' Dewhurst went out, leaving the door ajar.

Saxmundham, England

I

'Bloody Wednesday,' swore Lawrence Dingle. Market Day. That was why the traffic was moving so slowly. He leaned forward and switched off the radio, cutting off the droning bleat of the disc-jockey. It would take him ages to crawl through the town which would be packed with shoppers and slow-moving farm vehicles. 'Bloody hell,' he shouted as he rolled down his window. He would be late for his appointment in Ipswich.

The car in front, a red Ford, came to a halt to allow a tractor pulling a load of winter feed to enter the main road from a side-turning on the right. Dingle swore again and waved a fist at the courteous driver up ahead, calling him a variety of unimaginable names. The traffic edged forward at a snail's pace. Dingle was fuming.

II

The driver of the red Ford laughed to himself as he watched Dingle's tantrums in the rear-view mirror. Everything was set. He flicked on his transmitter. 'Foxtrot Two. Foxtrot Two. This is Foxtrot One. Over.'

'Receiving you, Foxtrot One. Over,' came the crackling reply.

'We're in position now. Repeat. We're in position. Over.'

'Roger, Foxtrot One. Proceed as planned. Foxtrot Two, over and out.'

III

Dingle only had himself to blame. On his fortnightly trips to the east coast union branches, he usually stayed overnight in Great Yarmouth and motored down on Tuesdays to Ipswich. Except when Sheila Keely put in an appearance. They had met last Christmas at a union bash: she worked as a secretary in the Seaman's Union. And she had taken a fancy to him, as he had to her. If she attended one of his mini-lectures on the Monday, that night and the next would be spent together discussing various aspects of international trade union solidarity in bed. And that meant being a day late in Ipswich, and a traffic jam through Saxmundham.

He beeped his horn in futile exasperation as the traffic ground to a halt which was only marginally slower, he decided, than it had been moving over the past few minutes. He gripped the steering wheel fiercely with both hands and swore again.

He was stopped on a short bend beneath the railway bridge and he could not see any further than the tractor. He knew there was a set of pedestrian lights just around the corner, then a set of traffic lights close by, and he guessed that the congestion would be greatest there.

The tractor crept forward, followed by the red Ford. Dingle let in the clutch a fraction. He could now see the pedestrian crossing. The tractor stopped. 'Damn,' he said. The traffic edged forward a few yards again.

Shoppers milled and spilled over the pavements and across the road, hurrying between the shops and market stalls on the right. Old world courtesy, thought Dingle, as he witnessed a barrel-chested gentleman stop and raise his hat to two old ladies who were standing at the lights. Baldy old coot, too, he grinned as he saw the bald pate exposed momentarily before the hat was reseated.

Dingle glanced away as the red Ford took off. A horn blared. He stalled his car.

He fumbled with the keys, accidentally slipped the car into second, stalled it again, all the time trying to keep his head low while out of the corner of his eye, he watched the man and the two ladies. He pulled forward and the traffic began to move more freely.

At the traffic lights, which conspired against him, he turned left then sharp left again into the free car park at the beginning of Leiston Road. He jumped out of the car, left it unlocked, and ran back to the corner. At the pedestrian crossing, he saw the man raise his hat again and cross the road. Dingle went in pursuit. The bald head was the giveaway. He had found Todor Zarev at last.

IV

Along Station Approach, past the Railway Hotel, across the level crossing, Zarev on one side of the road, Dingle on the other, two short, squat men, bobbing and weaving through the rush of shoppers.

Zarev turned right just after the second pub: Dingle recorded the landmarks and mentally sketched a map of the area. The crowds were thinning out so Dingle slowed his pace, but Zarev kept on, not looking back.

Left at the main road, fire station on the right, up towards a spread of detached houses, neatly obscured behind walls and the boughs of trees. Zarev entered the driveway of the third house. No gates, no number. Dingle kept on walking, noting the red post box that stood outside. He walked towards the tower which rose above the houses in the distance, retraced his route to confirm the landmarks, then returned to the house he had seen Zarev enter.

He walked past, and went next door. The house was hidden at the end of a curved drive, and two giant oaks stood sentry on either side, guarding the well-kept lawn and trimmed bushes. He rang the door bell.

A middle-aged woman answered. She smiled a welcome at Dingle.

'Mrs Braithwaite?' asked Dingle. The woman frowned. Dingle took a backwards step. 'Mrs Anne Braithwaite?' he added. He noted the blue rinse.

'I'm sorry,' said the woman. 'I think you have the wrong house.'

'I was told that Mr and Mrs Braithwaite lived here. I have an appointment.'

'I think you are mistaken. My name is Young.' She held the door open.

'Oh dear,' said Dingle. 'Perhaps next door?'

She shook her head. 'No. That way,' she said, pointing to the left. 'The Wolford sisters and their brother. And this way, the foreign gentleman. Polish, I think.' She smiled again. 'A rather difficult name to pronounce. It's Wrobovsky, or something like that. Lives on his own.'

'It does look as if I have the wrong address.'

'I can't recall anybody of that name in this area,' she said.

'Well thank you, Mrs Young, for your help.'

Dingle used the first phone box he came to. He had to get some change from the newsagents before he could call London. Tsanchev was in his office. They arranged to meet that night at the Embassy.

V

Dewhurst thanked Mrs Young for the use of her house. She was in her early twenties and was only too glad to be of help to the police. And of course she would not breathe a word of what had gone on that morning to anyone. She was aware that careless talk could jeopardize the police investigation into the ring of antique thieves operating in the area. It was in her own interest to see them brought to book: she had quite a few valuable pieces herself.

Dewhurst left the house through the tradesman's entrance accompanied by the middle-aged woman with the blue rinse. They walked up the main road towards the tower following the route that Dingle had taken earlier. They entered a tall, terraced house which gave an all-round view from the upstairs windows of the house where Zarev lived.

The nearest phone was in the kitchen. Dewhurst called his office, and asked to speak to Nike.

'Yes, Mr Dewhurst,' said Nike.

'Contact was made. Inform Sheila Keely that she must continue with her task, no matter how objectionable she may find it. I can't have Dingle becoming suspicious.'

'Yes,' said Nike.

Arkhangelskoye, Russia

Vadim cut across onto Gorky Street, circled round the back of the Byelorussian Railway Terminal and sped along Leningradsky Prospect. He passed under the tunnel into Volokolamskoye Chausseé, then forked left onto Petrova-Dalniye Chaussée, heading eastwards towards Ilyinskoye where his mother lived. It was Tuesday and the sun was shining.

He drove carefully as the roads were awash with the sludge of melting ice and snow. Other drivers gave his car, a black Volga, a wide berth once they saw the MOS registration plate of the Moscow City Council Garage which signified officialdom.

General Chebrikov had given him the day off to visit his widowed mother who was suffering from a heart complaint, and was confined to a wheelchair. On Monday evening he had shopped at the Food Shop on Dorogomilov-skaya Street and the boot of the Volga was crammed full with goodies from East and West which his mother would at first refuse, then reluctantly accept and then, with Vadim's help, pack away in cupboards and refrigerator with all the miserliness of a general preparing for a siege. Chebrikov had been kind enough to lend him his permit and had contributed a hundred dollars towards the binge.

About sixteen kilometres from Moscow, Vadim approached a vast walled estate overlooking the River Moskva. Formerly the home of Prince Golitsyn, it was now the People's Museum of Arkhangelskoye. The main buildings were set in parkland, and in the summer it was crowded with Muscovites and tourists as it was one of the most pleasant beauty spots close to the capital. But today, the museum was closed and the park was deserted.

At the main entrance to the estate, Vadim turned left and parked his car outside the Mozhaik restaurant. That, too, was closed, but there was a battered Zil saloon standing out front, its nose pointing towards Moscow.

General Lyalin, in mufti, sat at the table immediately inside the front door of the eatery, playing with a bunch of keys. In front of him was a leather-clad flask and a small silver tumbler next to an opened packet of Java cigarettes, and a gold Zippo lighter. Vadim noticed only one cigarette stub in the ash-tray.

'Good morning, Vadim Ivanovitch. And how was your journey?'

Vadim sat opposite the GRU chief. 'Pleasant enough,' he said. 'And yours?'

'Different. I am not used to driving myself. It can be dangerous when you are out of practice.'

Vadim recognized the veiled inference. 'I obeyed your instructions to the letter.'

'Were you followed?' asked Lyalin.

'No.'

'That's good, Vadim.' Lyalin lit up a cigarette. 'Yegenevi was behind you all the way,' he added. 'He insisted on being there just to be certain that Chebrikov was not suspicious about your visit to your mother. How is she, by the way?'

'No improvement,' Vadim murmured. He was shocked by the revelation that Lyalin's adjutant had tailed him all the way from the city without his knowing it.

'And you've stocked up with provisions for her?'

'Yes.' Vadim was nervous now.

'Good.' He dragged on the cigarette and let the smoke escape from his nostrils in two continuous streams. 'And what have you to tell me about Todor Zarev?'

Vadim sat forward eagerly, wishing to get the business over and done with as soon as possible. He assuaged the guilt he felt over the betrayal of his master with the thought that Lyalin and Chebrikov were, after all, both on the same side. And if his perfidy could also assist in keeping certain aspects of his private life from reaching the ears of General Chebrikov, then so much the better. 'Zarev's file was passed to General Chebrikov in May of last year.'

'That I know.' Lyalin poured himself a measure of vodka from the flask.

'Since then, there have been rumours that he went *swimming* in Europe on a top secret mission for the Premier.'

'Give me the facts.'

'Throughout June and July, Chebrikov was tense and bad-tempered. He held several meetings, mainly in secret, with the Premier and Fedorchuk, but what they were about I have no idea. He kept all the details locked in his private safe. I don't have access to it.'

'The old gang gets together again,' said Lyalin with a thin grin. 'Go on.'

'Then last week one of the *neighbours* reports that . . .'

'Which *neighbour* exactly?' said Lyalin.

'The Bulgarians. Radoslav Tsanchev in London.'

'I see.'

'Zarev was spotted in England. In Suffolk. A place called . . .'

'Here.' Lyalin handed over a note pad and pen which he took from his inside pocket. 'Write down the precise location.'

Vadim began to write. 'When the news came in, Chebrikov was away. It was on *Line DG*, so it came directly to his office. I saw it.' He gave back the pad and pen.

'What was Chebrikov's reaction?' Vadim was silent. 'Well, was he angry? Happy? What?' demanded Lyalin impatiently.

'I think he was angry because he was not there when the news came in. But he seemed pleased that Zarev had been located.'

'And you've no idea what Zarev was doing in England? Could he have defected?'

Vadim shook his head. 'No *mokrie dela* warrant was ever issued for Zarev. Department S, which oversees operations against defectors, was never informed about him. I checked all that out.'

'So,' said Lyalin. 'Zarev disappears for a year. On a mission, perhaps? Presumably in England. Then suddenly he surfaces. What's he been up to?' He tapped his chin with the index finger of his right hand.

'Chebrikov has had two meetings with the Premier and Fedorchuk since he learnt of Zarev's reappearance.'

'What is it that they know that I don't?' mused Lyalin. 'They have no right to keep me in the dark.' He stared at Vadim, but his mind was elsewhere. 'Todor Zarev. What can you tell me?' he mused.

Vienna, Austria

'I'll get this, Tony.' He doled out a pile of schillings onto the platter. The waiter, who had been standing in the wings, swooped on the money and scooped it away before he had a chance to double-check the amount.

Tony Ashburner grinned, showing the jagged edges of his nicotine-stained teeth. 'Over here, hawks and doves refers to the never-ending conflict between waiters and customers. If you ask him nicely when he returns, he'll bring you a swab for the scratches on the back of your hand.'

'That's the fastest I've seen him move all evening,' said Jimmy Capstick.

'A poor tip will see a world land speed record broken. He'll march us out of here faster than a Parisian whore can get her knickers off.' He poured the last of his cognac down his throat and smacked his lips appreciatively. 'Should we try one through in the bar?'

'Why not.' Capstick pushed back his chair. The waiter arrived and solicitously fussed him to his feet. 'Thanks,' he said. He slipped the man a couple of low denomination notes, which disappeared in a blur into a cavernous side-pocket, and followed Ashburner towards the exit.

In the background, a Joseph Lanner composition accompanied Ashburner and Capstick as they waltzed between the tightly packed tables laden with food and affluent Viennese.

In the bar, Capstick ordered the drinks which arrived just before the last of the ice melted in the glasses. 'Cheers,' said Capstick.

'They've never forgiven us for the war, you know,' said Ashburner. He lived up to his name by stubbing out his cigarette and immediately lighting another. 'They believe that if Britain hadn't been so stupid and gone to war over Poland, the Nazis could have had the war won in Europe, wiped out the Russians, and come to some sort of accommodation with Britain. They hate Churchill. They see the Cold War and the arms race as a direct consequence of British interference in Hitler's plans.' He blew a smoke-ring at Capstick which floated above his head like a minia-ture halo.

'I've heard it all before. They'll grow out of it one day.'

'I don't think so. There's a young generation growing up here, and in Germany, for whom the last war is simply another example of Zionist propaganda. They don't believe what happened in the camps.'

'They're in the minority. Small extremist groups.'

'They're growing very quickly. And their influence is spreading. They're using the opposition to the peace move-ment to push themselves centre stage.'

'Can't be all bad then, eh?' Capstick sounded bored. Ashburner got the message.

'So,' said Ashburner. 'The big day tomorrow. Moscow are coming clean over the Chernobyl disaster after six weeks of silence. Will this briefing be the first example of the Premier's much-vaunted *glasnost*, the nascent candour that he would have us believe is the new approach by the Kremlin? Or are we to witness the usual brick wall brief-ing?'

Ashburner had his back to the other customers in the bar. The piped music drowned any chance of eavesdropping.

Nevertheless, when Capstick spoke he raised his glass to his lips. 'Oleg Kovalevitsh will be in charge tomorrow.'

'The Head of Nuclear Safety?' Capstick nodded. 'Then they must be serious,' said Ashburner.

'I think so.' Capstick sipped his drink. 'You know he's KGB?'

'Never,' said Ashburner.

Capstick nodded. 'This is off the record, of course, Tony. But most of their top people in the nuclear industry are KGB. Have to be, what with all their emphasis on secrecy.'

'I see. But you still expect them to be open at the briefing?'

'Yes. And I think a lot will depend upon you and your colleagues in the press.' Capstick sat forward, his glass still raised. 'Look Tony. We've been getting persistent rumours from inside Russia that Chernobyl was no accident.'

'What? You mean . . .'

Capstick nodded slowly. 'Exactly. Sabotage.'

'Who by? Not by . . .'

'No. Not by us. At the moment we are not sure. But we don't want the finger of suspicion pointing our way.' Ashburner shook his head vigorously. 'There are enough dissidents inside Russia who could be responsible.'

'I suppose so.'

'The problem is we would like to know, and the Americans would too, the way the Russians are thinking. Is it all rumour, or was there sabotage at Chernobyl. And who do they think was responsible.'

Ashburner laughed nervously. 'You want me to put those questions at the briefing tomorrow?'

'Not directly. But you are an experienced newspaperman. You know how to ask the right type of question. You know, you ask one thing, but infer another. I've seen you in action. You're very good at it.'

Ashburner puffed out his chest. 'That's the reporter's art.'

'And as I said, you're very good at it,' replied Capstick. 'One or two of the American press contingent will be probing along the same lines. You can take your cues from each other. What we want to hear from the Russians is how much truth there is behind the rumours that Chernobyl was sabotage.'

'I think I can manage that. Even without the Americans,' he said dismissively.

'Great, Tony. You'll be doing yourself and Britain a big favour,' said Capstick, pleased with himself. Operation *Juniper* was progressing smoothly.

London, England

I

'There are fourteen nuclear power stations in operation in Britain today.'

'And how many of them are of the Magnox design?' asked Dewhurst.

'Nine, I think.' The Chief Scientific Officer of the United Kingdom Atomic Energy Authority considered his answer for a moment. 'Definitely nine,' he affirmed.

'And the station up at Sizewell is a Magnox?'

'Yes it is.' He gave Dewhurst a perplexed glance. 'Why Sizewell?'

'If you will bear with me for a few minutes,' said Dewhurst. 'It is a gas-cooled reactor, is it not?'

'Yes. Carbon dioxide to be precise.'

'And the loss of that coolant gas to the core could have very serious consequences for the integrity of both the fuel cans and the core itself?'

'Well. Yes.'

'As I understand it, should a sudden loss of coolant occur, the reactor would be shut down and emergency back-up cooling systems would intervene to counter any heat build-up in the fuel cans and the core.'

'That is the way the plant is designed: in-built redundancy systems which come into operation when there is a failure in one of the plant's main processes.'

The Chief Scientific Officer seemed confused by Dewhurst's questioning.

'And what would happen, if by chance, the emergency back-up systems were not intact?'

'Not intact? I don't understand.'

'What if they had been sabotaged, for example?'

Realization dawned. 'I see what you are driving at, Mr Dewhurst. Chernobyl and all that. The rumours of sabotage at the plant.'

'Precisely,' said Dewhurst. 'If the Russians suspect sabotage at Chernobyl, they probably will suspect that the West is to blame. Who knows?'

'True. True.' His eyes opened wide in horror. 'Revenge,' he whispered. 'They might retaliate.'

'I wouldn't put it past them.'

'And you think Sizewell might be the target?'

'Just an educated guess,' said Dewhurst. 'We often get reports of Russian submarines operating off the east coast. It would be very easy to . . .'

'I understand,' he said. 'Say no more.'

'But the cooling systems, including the back-ups, would be the ideal targets in the event of a sabotage attempt?'

'Most definitely.'

II

Nike bit into the ham sandwich. A few crumbs dropped onto the report he was reading. He shook them away. Most of the MI6 networks inside Russia, he read, had been betrayed to the KGB by Leonard Binder in order to convince the Soviet leadership that the information about the traitor *Cedar* was authentic. Now Binder was Head of

Russia Section, having replaced the late Joseph Mercer who had originally set up the networks.

Only two of them remained. And one of them, code-named *Solicitor*, was based in Kiev. It couldn't be better, he thought. Luck? Coincidence? No. Not at all. Nike didn't believe in either. It was the *Grand Design*. And Mr Dewhurst was in contact with it.

It had been Mr Dewhurst who had plucked Nike from the nomadic obscurity of his life of petty crime, and who had revealed to him what he was truly destined to be: a man to fear and loathe; a ruthless, merciless killing machine. Nike enjoyed the terror he generated in his victims and his colleagues: it gave him power. He was the grim reaper. 'Ruthless. Merciless,' he whispered. He loved that description of himself. They were Mr Dewhurst's words: he had given them to him. They were Nike's battle honours, linguistic medals.

He finished his lunch and brushed away the remaining crumbs. He pressed the bell and the secretary entered the cubicle a few seconds later. He asked her for the file on the *Solicitor* network. He knew it off by heart, and had a mental image of the four individuals: he wanted one more glimpse before setting off for Kiev, just to put them finally and irrevocably in his power.

Mr Dewhurst had power, too. One word from him and MI6 had opened all their doors. Nike had access to everything. Mr Dewhurst had spoken. Operation *Juniper* had top priority.

III

'It's *Rioja*,' said Julia. She had placed the glass of wine in Maitland's hand as soon as he stepped over the threshold, and then she had given him a kiss before retreating to the kitchen.

'It's fine,' said Maitland. He took off his coat, draped it over the back of a chair, and switched on the television. He yawned.

Julia emerged, crept up behind him and circled his waist with her arms. She pecked him on the back of the neck. 'Good trip?' she asked.

'So so,' he said. He put one arm behind him and squeezed her buttocks. 'I still can't see why I had to go.'

'Never mind. It's over now.' She rested her head between his shoulders, and moved her hands down to his groin.

'That's nice,' he whispered hoarsely. He had spent a whole week on Dewhurst's instructions in Belfast examining the arms and explosives caches that the RUC had uncovered in the last year, and which they had stored in two barracks. Then just before he was due to leave, he was ordered to organize the shipment to England of all the impounded *Semtex* plastic explosive. Almost two tons of the stuff. It had been a nightmare, what with all the paperwork, documentation, and transportation, on both sides of the Irish Sea; and Dewhurst's failure to come through with the necessary authority despite the bureaucratic mountains that had to be overcome. What a week. He was so tired.

'Have you been following that?' asked Julia. She was watching the television, her head resting on his arm. 'The talk of sabotage at Chernobyl?'

'Some of it. Haven't had the time really. Probably just the press trying to sell extra copy.'

'I don't think so. That Russian scientist, Kovalevitsh, got pretty flustered the other day during his press conference when the matter was put to him. I think the Russians suspect sabotage.'

Maitland deposited his glass on the television set, turned, and broke her hold. He pulled her to him and kissed her neck. 'Never mind that now,' he mumbled. He nibbled her ear.

'What about the curry?' she asked, squirming with pleasure. Her voice was husky and her eyes glinted with passion.

'They say curries should be eaten the day after they're cooked, don't they?'

IV

'I will brief the Joint Intelligence Committee myself,' said MacKenzie.

'As you wish,' said Dewhurst.

'Nothing in writing. A verbal summary only.'

Dewhurst had to smile. If Operation *Juniper* went well, MacKenzie would receive all the accolades. If it failed, there would be nothing in writing to compromise him. He would refer all criticisms to his Operations Chief. 'All the action will take place in a small area of East Suffolk, around the towns of Aldeburgh, Leiston and Saxmundham. Todor Zarev is in place there.'

'And Leiston is right next door to the Sizewell nuclear power station,' said MacKenzie.

'Exactly. A group of Russians have been lured into the area in the hope of retrieving Zarev. Explosives will be found at certain critical locations at Sizewell. The Russians will be captured nearby as they make their escape with Zarev. The inference for public consumption is that the Russians, or *Spetsnaz*, were attempting to blow up Sizewell in retaliation for Chernobyl, which the Western press has been hyping as sabotage, based on rumours emanating from inside Russia.'

'With us as the alleged perpetrators?'

'Yes. So it will be seen in Britain as an unjustified retaliation. But, most importantly, in the light of the Kiev action, the Russian people will see it as justified revenge.'

'Is that all there is then, to *Juniper*?'

'Refer the JIC to Bernhardt's memo. *Brave Defender* did nothing to alert the public to a conventional Russian threat. This exercise will. Public perspectives will change. The peace movement will be undermined.'

'It will certainly relieve the pressure on the President to sit down and talk disarmament with the Russians if they can be shown to be so despicable.'

'Indeed. It will also make the public aware that despite the Russian drive for negotiations, they can never be trusted. Russian inspired peace talks will be seen simply as a smoke-screen to cover their continuing hostile activities against the West.'

Kiev, Russia

I

Kiev was the earliest capital of a recognizable Russian state, a position it held until the thirteenth century when it was overrun and destroyed by the Golden Horde of Genghis Khan. During the Second World War, Kiev was again razed to the ground, this time by the German hordes, and though rebuilt and reconstructed under Stalin, many fine historical sites and shrines were lost to the world forever.

The city lies on both sides of the River Dnieper, the third longest river in Europe, and one of the main waterways of the Soviet Union. The right bank of the river is hilly, while the left is flat and even, composed of the rich arable soil that makes the Ukraine Soviet Socialist Republic, of which Kiev is the capital, the bread basket of Russia.

Nike waited outside the Central Railway Station until the station clock said quarter to six. Then he walked down the steps to join the queue at the trolley-bus stop.

He was dressed in dirty, blue dungarees, and wore a pair of cheap, black labourer's boots on his feet. Under his left arm he carried two pieces of black bread and a long piece of Polish sausage bundled together in a sheet of newspaper. He boarded the bus with the other passengers and dropped a ten kopec piece into the machine by the driver and received a brown ticket in return.

The trolley-bus was only half full so he chose a seat near to the exit, sat down, and closed his eyes. The evacuation of the city's children was proceeding smoothly as far as he could tell from the three hours he had spent hanging around the station. But he could see in the faces of the adult population the tension and the strain that the Chernobyl disaster had wrought. The day had been warm, with the temperature in the high sixties, but the streets, even during the early evening rush hour, had been very quiet. Where old men would sit and reminisce, where young lovers would linger among the blooms of spring, and where the housewife would stand and barter, Nike had witnessed a void. The city was scared.

At the main Post Office on Kreshchatik, he got off and crossed the road to the Hotel Dnieper. Normally, at this time of the year, Intourist's showpiece hotel would be packed to overflowing with tourists from all over the world. But its portals were deserted and the taxi-rank was empty.

He walked west, along the Street of Revolutionary Heroes, slowing his pace to a stroll when a clock in front of a clothing store told him he was ahead of time. He ambled left into Chelyuskintsev Street, down past the Planetarium, and into Kalinin Square. Now he was behind time according to the clock in the square, so he hurried on, and into Bogdan Khmelnitsky Square, and paused for a moment to get his bearing beneath the gigantic statue of the Cossack Hetman. A convoy of Militia trucks swept by, while overhead, a distant helicopter whirred its way north to the stricken reactor site.

Behind the statue, Nike saw the dome of Saint Sophia's cathedral and he walked across to the precinct whose blue and white tiled pavement glistened in the setting sun. The cathedral was now a museum, and he read the notice-boards for five minutes as instructed before heading off again.

He wasn't sure of the time now, and he cursed the *Solicitor* network for their pedantic, time-wasting instructions. The security services would be too busy in and around Chernobyl to bother him, but *Solicitor* had insisted on checks and double-checks for this trip. He had not looked behind once throughout his journey, but he had no doubt that every stage had been covered by a member of *Solicitor*.

The street led into a small garden which contained the Golden Gate, once part of Kiev's ancient fortifications. He found the seat, number eleven, and he sat down and began to eat.

The bread was dry and stuck to the roof of his mouth: the sausage was heavily laced with garlic and contained more gristle than meat. He spat out bits of the tougher pieces from time to time, the last one landing on the toecap of a shoe which suddenly appeared in his vision.

The shoe was one of a pair, dark brown with a short heel, and their owner was a young woman in her early thirties, with fair hair and a round, cherubic face encased in a floral scarf. She wore a blouson and a red flared skirt, exactly what Nike had been told to expect.

She began the *parole*. 'Excuse me, comrade. I seem to have lost my way. Could you direct me to the Opera House?'

'I'm sorry,' replied Nike. 'I am a stranger in Kiev. I've only just arrived from Belaya Tserkov to assist in the emergency.' His Russian was rusty and he had problems with some of the consonants, so that he seemed to stutter his words.

'It is a tragedy for the Ukraine and her people.'

'It is a tragedy for the world,' finished Nike.

She sat down beside him, and he broke off a bit of bread from the piece he was holding. She took it and popped it into her mouth and chewed it slowly. She refused Nike's offer of Polish sausage with a shake of her head. 'We will go in a few minutes.'

'Where to?' he asked, carefully re-wrapping the last piece of bread and the remainder of the sausage.

'Darnitsa,' she said, pointing eastwards. 'An industrial sprawl, full of chemical factories, machine shops and workers' flats.'

II

The woman's name was Tanya and she worked for the Ministry of Agricultural Machinery in Kiev. She was highly thought of in the Ministry, and had access to all the major discussions and decisions, as well as travel both at home and abroad. Tanya was the leader of the *Solicitor* network.

She took him to a low, modern apartment block on Mayakovsky Street where she shared a flat with her brother, Filip, on the third floor. She rang a code on the bell at the front entrance before entering, and they rode the elevator up to the apartment where Filip was waiting for them. He worked as an engineer in a pharmaceutical laboratory, and the first thing he did was to press some iodine tablets into Nike's hand and insist that he take them right away. Nike obliged, without telling him he had already dosed himself before entering the country.

The other two members of *Solicitor* were Igor and Sergei. Igor was the radio operator, a chain-smoker, who soon filled the room with dense layers of smoke. Sergei was the last to arrive, after dark. He was a tall, thin, nervous man who worked as a technician at the Chernobyl reactor site. He had just finished his shift and was on his way home when the disaster had occurred. He had not been back since. His nervousness was due to his fear of the KGB, who, he thought, would be out searching for him because of his continued absence. Filip spent some time assuring him that he would be safe at least until they had the melt-down fully under control.

They talked well into the night, Tanya and Filip explaining to Nike the workings of the network, and questioning him on how well their intelligence was received in London. Nike answered as little as he could, claiming that he was tired and that the morning would be more appropriate for discussion. Both Sergei and Igor, who had been nodding off for some time, agreed and Igor suggested they should get some sleep.

The apartment was well-appointed but tiny. The two bedrooms were not much bigger than the beds they contained, and the living room and kitchen were equally as small. The toilet was an afterthought, grafted onto the kitchen, next to the balcony that overlooked a building site.

During the conversation, Nike had slumped into the corner of the settee, and he insisted that he slept where he was. Filip and Sergei went to one bedroom, while Tanya and Igor took the other. Within minutes, the flat was silent. Nike waited an hour before he made his move.

He had casually slipped his newspaper-wrapped parcel under the coffee-table out of the way upon first entering the apartment. Now he took it out and pulled away the paper. He broke open the Polish sausage and extracted the detonator which he cleaned carefully. Then he began to squeeze the black bread into a ball: it did not crumble, and in a few seconds he placed the ball of *RD-X* plastic explosive on the table top.

His boots were at the side of the settee. He pulled out the right lace and stripped the ends to expose the detonator cord, and attached it to the explosive. From his pocket he took a piece of string, re-laced his boots, and put them on. He found his pencil flashlight and penknife in the breast pocket of his dungarees, and, with the explosive and detonator in the other hand, he tiptoed into the hallway.

The bell mechanism was on the wall between the two bedroom doors. He listened at both and heard a gentle snoring. He lifted off the outer casing of the electric bell and crept into the bathroom. He turned on the water geyser without igniting the gas jet. A hissing sound filled the room. He left the door open and moved through into the kitchen where he turned on the main oven and the gas rings, leaving the door ajar into the hallway. Silently he eased open both bedroom doors, then attached the explosive and detonator cord to the bell. He let himself out of the apartment as stealthily as he could.

He walked down to the entrance hall and waited a few minutes. The building was deathly still. He went outside and pressed the bell for Tanya's flat.

The blast sent a tongue of flame scorching across the balcony and into the street. The whole block shook and masonry and debris clattered to the ground. Nike was off and running, seeking shelter in the deep shadows of the building site.

III

'This way,' said Colonel Lessiovsky.

Chebrikov was perspiring freely. The climb to the top floor of the block of flats had taken its toll. He paused and leant against the banister, trying to get his breath back.

Lessiovsky stopped outside the flat and said a few words to the KGB crew and the Militiamen who were guarding the entrance.

He looked down into the well of the staircase and was greeted by a sea of upturned faces, young and old alike, their lips moving as they broadcast the latest turn of events to their neighbours.

Lessiovsky went inside and Chebrikov reluctantly followed.

The living room smelt of boiled cabbage and rotten plaster. Lessiovsky was talking to a KGB captain who stood over an elderly woman sitting in a corner.

'His mother didn't say a word,' the captain reported. 'As soon as she saw me at the door she took me directly to the hiding place. A false floor in the wardrobe in his bedroom.'

Chebrikov had moved on into the bedroom. Two KGB officers from the Technical Support Unit were down on their knees in front of the wardrobe examining the cache. They had already removed the radio and a pile of *one-time* pads. Lessiovsky entered and tapped him on the shoulder.

'What should we do with the old lady?' he whispered.

'Leave her for now. We have the whole network.' He sat down on the edge of the bed. The muscles in his legs felt stiff and weary. He watched the two men at their task, uncovering the traces of Igor Ilouye's treachery.

Late last night in Moscow he had received a *Line DG* communiqué from the London resident, Pitovranov. Binder, the KGB mole inside MI6, had finally made contact again. He had supplied details of Mercer's two remaining networks inside Russia: *Teacher* in Vladivostock; *Solicitor* in Kiev. It was because of Chernobyl, and all the implications therefrom, that he had flown to Kiev this morning to investigate personally the *Solicitor* spy ring. And of course to see if there was a chance of uncovering *Cedar*.

'Code book,' said one of the technicians. He held it up by one corner as if it was a piece of shit and dropped it into a transparent polythene envelope. Colonel Lessiovsky asked for it to be handed over.

Chebrikov fingered the side pocket of his tunic; it contained Pitovranov's message. On arrival at Kiev, he had walked in on the Darnitsa bombing and the four badly burnt bodies. He had immediately recognised the address of the brother and sister in Mayakovsky Street. He had ordered Lessiovsky to send his men to the other two addresses that Pitovranov had supplied. Igor Ilouye had been the radio operator for the *Solicitor* group.

But what had caused the explosion in the flat? Had the gang been preparing an explosive device that had been accidentally detonated? Or had the British eliminated them? But why? Because they were in danger of being betrayed? But that would only make sense if the *Solicitor* network had some secret that could compromise the British if it ever came out.

The Western press had been rumour-mongering about sabotage at Chernobyl. Now those rumours took on a greater significance in the light of the Darnitsa explosion. Russians lived on a diet of gossip and hearsay. It would not be long before the rumour-mongers would connect Chernobyl and Darnitsa. Sabotage would again be on everybody's lips. British sabotage? And the Western press would soon pick it up.

Moscow, Russia

I

Fedorchuk had the *Satsivi*, young, fresh chicken in a spicy sauce; Chebrikov chose the *Osetrina na vertelye*, spit-roasted sturgeon. The Aragvi restaurant on Gorky Street specialized in Georgian cuisine. And discreet, private rooms.

'It is a provocation, Vitaly,' said Chebrikov. 'The Premier agrees.'

Fedorchuk was not convinced. 'For what reason, Viktor?'

'Since when do the British need a reason? We did not start the rumours of sabotage at Chernobyl. We did not eliminate the *Solicitor* network.' He forked a piece of fish into his mouth and swallowed almost immediately. 'I believe the British want us to think that they did indeed sabotage Chernobyl.'

'But why?'

Chebrikov shrugged. 'Have you seen what the British have down in that area?'

'You mean in East Suffolk where they're holding Zarev?'

Chebrikov bit into a fat, red Bulgarian tomato. 'There's Lakenheath and Mildenhall. American nuclear bases. There are nuclear weapons buried in silos along the runways.' He pushed his plate to one side. 'And then on the coast, there's Sizewell and Bradwell. Nuclear power stations.'

'I've seen the maps, Viktor.'

'Good. And if we were to send a team to bring out Zarev on the very slim chance, I believe, that he knows the identity of *Cedar*, and if any of our men were detected even within a hundred miles of one of those installations, captured alive, then what would be the outcome? The British would have a field day. Can you imagine what they would make of it, how they would play it up? Revenge attack. Saboteurs caught in the act. The *Spetsnaz* strike. No. We couldn't have that, Vitaly.' Chebrikov was sweating. He hated these private rooms. But Fedorchuk had insisted. When he ate out, part of the pleasure was the company of other diners. Here, in their privacy, he was cut off and isolated as he was when he was in his own office. He undid his tie and opened the top button of his shirt.

'You are assuming that the British have set up Zarev with the sole intention of luring us into Suffolk,' said Fedorchuk. 'And even if they have, I still think the chance is worth taking if it means we may uncover *Cedar*'s identity.'

'The Premier does not see it that way. The odds are against us. The risk is too great. The arms control talks must proceed. They would be endangered by another raid into England. It would jeopardize all the Premier's hopes and aspirations and give the West another reason not to talk to us. And if the Premier doesn't wring some concessions from the West, he will further weaken his own position in the Kremlin. His enemies will be encouraged to move against him.'

II

Lyalin had switched off the lights and opened all the blinds. The road lamps and the headlights of the passing traffic on Znamensky Street illuminated his office, projecting shadowy patterns along the walls and among the furniture, while drawing sharp edges and lines across the ceiling, a colourless kaleidoscope, which gave him the sensation that he was slowly moving through a darkened tunnel.

He sat in the corner near the bookcase, his chair pushed back onto two legs, his feet barely touching the carpet, his shoulders and head resting against the wall. His tunic was undone, the pockets bulged with his hands, and his tie hung like a noose around his thick neck. Flecks of ash littered his shirt front, while at his feet, ground into the carpet, were the stubs of several cigarettes.

The main nuclear arms test site at Semipalatinsk had been quiet for a year now, but the Premier's unilateral test ban had not been taken up by the Americans. So far, all the Premier's overtures for arms reduction had been treated with distrust and disdain by the West. The Star Wars project was proceeding and further deployments of missiles in Europe were continuing. Then there was the attack on Libya and the implied threat to Russia not to interfere by the missile movements in Britain, Italy and Germany.

The Kremlin rumour-machine had it that several members of the Politburo were disillusioned with the Premier; not only had all his efforts to negotiate with the West resulted in failure, but he was circumventing the consultative procedure of the Politburo and making proposals to the West that had not been discussed or agreed upon. Speculation was that the Premier was trying to become a one-man show, that he was trying to move too far, too quickly, and not getting anywhere at all.

Lyalin agreed in principle with the Premier's basic aims of reducing arms spending so that more cash would be available to the social reform programmes. The country was in a very difficult time of its development.

But on the other hand, Lyalin could sympathise with his colleagues in the Army High Command who saw the Premier's headlong pursuit of an arms deal with the West without proper consultation as a danger to Russia's security.

He was caught in the middle. But as the Premier's initiatives failed and as the military demanded more finances to compete with the Americans, the time was drawing closer when he would have to decide which side to support. And if he chose incorrectly, he would lose his power, his position and his one great hope of being elected to the highest organ of government in Russia, the Politburo.

He had to make the choice now. The Premier. Or the hawks.

Todor Zarev. He had an instinct that this man could be of help. If he knew what Zarev knew, then perhaps he could make the right decision. He might even be able to influence one side or the other, become the power broker inside the Kremlin.

Zarev was the key. He was certain.

He pushed himself off the wall and stood up.

'Yegeveni,' he shouted. 'Yegeveni.'

Leather boots striding hurriedly across the polished floor outside was the response. The door opened admitting a wedge of bright light which caused the shadows to disperse.

'Comrade General,' enquired Yegeveni, glancing round the room.

'I want Colonel Talebov in my office first thing in the morning,' ordered Lyalin.

'But Comrade General. He's at Wrangle Island.'

'I don't care if he's on the moon. Get him here.' He

went over to his desk and switched on the map. 'Well? What are you waiting for? Get moving.'

Yegeveni hesitated for a moment. 'Yes, Comrade General.' He hurried out.

Aldeburgh, England

I

'Do you remember the old Norman 266 coastal motor cruisers?' asked Penfield.

'No. Not really,' said Talebov shaking his head.

Penfield was disappointed. 'They were the best. Don't get me wrong,' he added quickly as he saw the expression on Talebov's face. 'The Atlanta is every bit as good. In fact, it's based on the Norman design. See the flare on the hull's forward section. The Norman didn't have that. Improves the boat's seakeeping.'

Penfield helped Talebov on board. 'What's she fitted with?'

'Twin petrol Volvo Pentas, giving about 290 horse power and up to thirty knots,' said Penfield, directing him to the bridge. 'Coachroof.' He pointed upwards. 'Ideal for sunbathing.'

'Not in this weather,' said Talebov. He gave the radio a quick examination. It would do.

'It'll get better. Mark my words. Let's go below.'

'How many can she sleep?'

'Four adults. See. Open plan. You've got the two Vee berths. Then there's the double in the convertible dinette.' Penfield guided his tenant forward. 'Galley and toilet-cum-shower through there.'

'Very nice,' said Talebov trying to show his enthusiasm. He could see that Penfield had all day to spare and would

161

use most of it in describing every feature of the vessel. But Talebov wanted to get the formalities over and done with. He had much more important business elsewhere.

'You down for the Festival?' asked Penfield.

'Yes. About two weeks or so.' Talebov climbed back up on deck.

'And you'll want the boat for all that time?'

'I was thinking of three weeks.' Talebov could see the greed in Penfield's demeanour. 'Just in case I have to stay over a few extra days.'

'That shouldn't present any problems.'

Talebov glanced across to Ferry Point, then down the river to the Yacht Club, and beyond that to the Martello Tower. 'I'll pay in advance. In cash,' he said.

'That'll be fine,' said Penfield. He rubbed his hands together. 'And what about mooring? You'll keep her here?'

'I was thinking of further up river. Pettit's dock, perhaps.'

'That's fine with me. Look, why don't we have some lunch. And a pint or two. Then, this afternoon, I'll take you down the river. Show you how she goes. Then tomorrow, I can meet you in town and we can draw up an agreement, get the insurance sorted out, and then she'll be all yours.'

'Sounds fine by me,' said Talebov.

'Great. Thank you very much, Mr Buckner,' said Penfield.

II

Talebov had arrived in England two days ago, flying into Heathrow on a West German passport. The formalities

162

were short and superficial, his reason for visiting the country, the thirty-ninth Aldeburgh Festival of Music and the Arts, was accepted without question. His hire car, a BMW 735, was awaiting him after the process of customs, and he had set out for Aldeburgh beneath a darkening sky, arriving in time for lunch.

He had to spend a couple of nights in lodgings before he finally struck up the deal with Penfield for the lease of the *River Queen*, and now, ensconced aboard the twenty-seven footer, he began to put the final touches to his plans.

He had already made a swift reconnaissance of the house and Saxmundham, and he intended paying another visit later that night. He had all the details of the place together with a breakdown of Zarev's probable movements over the next few days. Zarev appeared to have become a creature of habit, which to his way of thinking, and knowing the man's record, was very surprising. Could a man who had lived most of his life by his wits, operating undercover in strange countries, constantly poised for the unexpected, compelled by survival to irregularity and unpredictability, quickly settle down to a life of mundane routine which suppressed those very instincts? Talebov could not help wondering that there was a lot more to this mission than Lyalin suspected: he promised caution and discretion; he suspected a hidden hand. But whose?

He dined at the Wentworth: he was lucky, there had been a cancellation, and the hotel management prided itself on accommodating foreign visitors. The waitress showed him to a table in the long, narrow section of the dining room, almost beneath the archway that led into the square annexe. He sat with his back to the majority of diners, though the three tables in front of him, full of diamonds, accents and freshly coiffured hair, afforded him sufficient diversions during the course of his meal. A constant hum of prattle formed the backdrop to the incessant clack of knives and forks against china plates, and the scuff of dashing feet as the waitresses nimbly skipped between tables and kitchen.

He ordered soup, a medium sirloin and the red house wine, then tucked into the crisp bread roll. Snatches of conversation assailed him, his ears like antennae, automatically probing the ether. He tried to concentrate on what he had to do over the next few days, but he found himself dwelling on the past, on the twists and turns in his life that had led him to this place.

This was his second visit to England: his first had been in the early seventies when he was attached to the Embassy as a Commercial Attaché, a very thin disguise for his true role as second in command of the GRU contingent. From London, he had been promoted to Washington, and he would have been there yet but for the intervention of the Afghanistan problem.

He had been born in Azerbaydzhan and had grown up there among a babble of languages and dialects. During his Military Service, his flair for languages had come to the attention of the GRU who had swept him up into their ranks. He had seen duty in Iran, Syria and Turkey, and had been a natural choice for the mission inside Afghanistan. Not only could he speak the native dialects, but his complexion, when exposed to the sun, was the same coffee-colour as the natives. He had blended well into his surroundings.

But he had hated Afghanistan, loathed it. The dust, the filth, the brutal ignorance of the tribesmen, and their adherence to the outmoded creed that condemned their womenfolk to a life of slavery and drudgery.

When Lyalin had offered him the chance to return to

Russia to work on a top secret project, he had leapt at it. He was to be chief instructor to the *Spetsnaz* which Lyalin, as head of the GRU, was to command, much to the chagrin of the rival KGB.

He had hardly begun the task when Lyalin had peremptorily summoned him to Moscow for the mission to England, to bring out Todor Zarev, a Bulgarian, who had attained the rare distinction of holding a Colonel's commission in the KGB.

Talebov had not been told the reason why, nor did he query it: he simply followed orders, as he had done all his life. Lyalin wanted Zarev before the KGB could get their hands on him. Talebov would get him as ordered.

Even though the initial, preparatory phases of the mission were hurried and brief, he felt sure he had covered himself and had laid the groundwork for a successful conclusion. The other three members of the *boyevaya*, the combat group, would be arriving sometime tomorrow. He had selected them himself from the first intake of GRU operatives for training as *Spetsnaz*. They were the best. The two men would arrive in Great Yarmouth by ferry from Scheveningen; the woman would come into Gatwick, and then travel to the rendezvous from Battersea Helipad aboard a Sikorsky 76.

Tomorrow evening they would meet up as tourists at the ruins of Leiston Abbey and then move down to headquarters to finalize their plans aboard the *River Queen*.

III

All his senses were suddenly alert and wide-awake: sleep had rapidly evaporated. Talebov did not move. There it was again. A gentle rocking of the boat as if someone had stealthily climbed aboard. Slowly, Talebov slipped a hand under his pillow and found the handle of the hunting knife he had bought in Aldeburgh on his arrival. The boat heaved once more, and the tranquil lap of water against the boards was more pronounced. He pulled out the knife and swung his feet to the deck. A timid tapping on the hatch: he crept forward and released the catch.

The hatch swung open and a hand appeared. Talebov grabbed it and heaved it over his shoulder. The rest of the body followed. It landed with a crashing thud close to the bunk.

Talebov drove both his knees into the man's back, heard the blast of exhausting lungs, then grabbed a handful of hair, pulling the head back to expose the white neck to the silvery gleam of the knife.

'Aaagh. No,' wailed the man.

'Talk to me,' said Talebov.

'Buckner. It's me. Whiston.'

'I can't hear you,' said Talebov and pressed the knife deeper into the throat.

'Mozart. Mozart,' he gasped. '*Quintet in C*. Wednesday.'

'You're early,' said Talebov withdrawing the blade. He sank down onto the bunk bed. Whiston struggled to his feet, adjusting his clothing.

'There was no need for that,' he whined sulkily.

'Procedures and *paroles*. Didn't they drum that into you during training? They are the difference between life and death.' Whiston was one of the team of GRU agents who had been observing Zarev and his home, and also laying the groundwork for Talebov's mission.

'I brought the golf clubs,' he said.

'Bring them down, then.'

Whiston went back on deck and soon returned amid a

166

series of bumps and thuds carrying two Wilson Satellite golf bags, each containing a set of used Slazenger clubs. He dumped them at Talebov's feet, and stood there waiting.

'Well?' asked Talebov.

'Don't you want any help?' replied Whiston.

'No thanks.' He stared at Whiston, silently telling him to go. Whiston left without another word.

The first bag of clubs he emptied contained the ammunition. The second held four Uzi machine pistols. Talebov was ready to go.

London, England

I

Maitland was trying to think about Barcelona. It was Friday and he had been due to fly out there with Julia on Sunday for three weeks' holiday. But Dewhurst had put an end to all that.

'It will mean a delay of four days at the most. The Department will defray any additional costs,' said Dewhurst.

'And I'm just to observe?'

'Yes. This has nothing to do with Operations as such. But Sir Robert has insisted on a representative being present. I'm sorry, Oliver, but you're the only senior officer I have left.'

Maitland picked up the briefing report and opened it. 'Special Branch and Jimmy Capstick's team?' Operation *Juniper*, he read.

'They've got men everywhere. They've set up headquarters in a large house in Aldeburgh, Victoria Road, to be precise. But there's no need for you to stay there. I've booked you a room at the Wentworth. A double.' He smiled knowingly. 'And I've also got some spare tickets for the English Chamber Orchestra at Snape Maltings. You may as well enjoy yourself while you're up there.'

When Dewhurst was pleasant, thought Maitland, it was only because he wanted something done. When he distributed largesse, that something usually spelt trouble. 'It could be a false alarm, couldn't it?'

168

'Indeed, yes. But we have to follow it through. It wouldn't look very good, would it, if we ignored it, and then something did happen at Sizewell? Not in the wake of Chernobyl, eh?'

'True enough,' said Maitland as he read the brief. A group of anti-nuclear power activists were planning an assault on the Sizewell nuclear power station some time in the next few days. It was all tied in to the disaster in Russia and what the activists saw as the complacency of the authorities to the question of safety and security at British nuclear installations.

'In a way, something like this was bound to happen,' said Dewhurst.

'I suppose so,' said Maitland. He had decided to take Julia with him. After all there was a double room, and two concert tickets for each night.

II

Nike and Dewhurst stood over the scale drawings of the Sizewell plant. 'These four points in red,' said Nike. 'If they were simultaneously destroyed then the whole cooling process to the fuel cans and the core, including the emergency back-up systems, would cease altogether.'

'Fine,' said Dewhurst.

'Green indicates the four entry points where the outer fence will be breached. The orange lines show the paths the saboteurs would take to reach their objectives in red, thereby avoiding the security sweeps.'

Dewhurst sat down. 'Have you moved the *Semtex*, yet?'

'It arrived at the house in Saxmundham this morning, together with the pouches.'

'With Russian markings?'

'Yes,' said Nike.

'Okay. Maitland should be at Aldeburgh now. There's nothing more for you to do down here. I should be there in the next day or so.' Dewhurst took off his spectacles and started to polish them. 'Watch Maitland like a hawk. And remember. *Nacht und Nebel.*' Nike's broad grin reminded him of an open tomb. '*Rückkehr Ungewünscht,*' he added malevolently.

III

Nike drove himself to Aldeburgh. Maitland would soon be a dead man. Mr Dewhurst had decreed it. He entertained himself on the long journey toying with the various ways he could dispose of the troublesome Maitland.

Nacht und Nebel. Trust Mr Dewhurst to come up with something like that. *Night and Fog.* Words from the German epic poem, the Nibelungenlied. The Nazis appended those words next to the names of those who were to disappear into the camps as non-persons. Sometimes the methodical Nazis also added *Rückkehr Ungewünscht* to the names: *return not desired.* It was the death sentence.

Maitland was a dead man already. He just did not know it.

IV

Dewhurst walked down a flight of stairs to Capstick's room.

'We think we've got him,' said Gregson. On the wall behind the door was an array of photographs. Some had been taken in daylight, others at night. All of them had been snapped from the top floor of the house close to the tower in Saxmundham from which Capstick's men kept Zarev's residence under observation.

'Let me see,' said Dewhurst.

'This was the first one. Early afternoon.' He took down the photograph and gave it to Dewhurst. 'The time is on the back. The second was late last night. Infra-red shot. It's a bit blurred. But no doubt it's the same man.'

Dewhurst compared the likenesses. 'Okay.'

'This one this morning. It only arrived a few hours ago.' He handed over the third shot to Dewhurst. 'I passed it on to Records straight away. And this is what they came up with.' He went across to Capstick's desk.

'Someone we know?' asked Dewhurst expectantly.

'You bet. Kauffman in Records is very good at this sort of thing.' Gregson took the snaps from Dewhurst and lined them up on the desk. From a folder he produced a fourth. 'Talebov. Stanislav Dimitrevich. GRU Captain as was.'

Dewhurst inspected the pictures closely. 'Yes,' he said finally. 'Lost some hair, gained a few wrinkles. But the same man.'

'London. Then Washington. That's where we first picked him up. Dropped out of sight in 1979.'

'Not KGB?'

'Definitely GRU. Here's his record. Langley are sending over what they know about him.'

Dewhurst tapped the desk top. 'GRU,' he repeated, gazing out of the window. 'Why not KGB?'

Aldeburgh, England

I

Constable Worter was uncomfortable: he was wearing civilian clothes while on duty. It didn't seem right or proper. As he sat in the car, he prayed that he would not be recognized by any of the locals: he could imagine what the wags would have to say about him being out of uniform, particularly when they heard about the men from London.

That was another thing that irked him: why were they here? And why was he acting as their chauffeur? Admittedly, he was not overburdened by his duties and had the time to help the men from London. But Aldeburgh was crime-free. As a serving officer in the area, he had not had to make an arrest in four years. So what had warranted the intrusion by these big city policemen?

Everything was hush hush. A photograph of a man had been circulated to all officers. Find him, the Inspector had said. Use the local newspapers to see who was offering accommodation, on land and on water. Check with them. Had any of them leased a property or a boat to the man in the picture? Keep it all low key. No uniforms. As if that mattered.

He had decided to check out the boat owners: they usually made a killing letting off their craft during the summer to tourists and holiday-makers. So he had started with his uncle, Robin Penfield. As luck would have it, he immediately recognized the man. The Inspector had been overjoyed, relieved, too. But then the men from London took over. They did not say a lot, just like on the television, playing their cards close to the chest.

So, here he was. Parked outside his uncle's home, while his uncle was being interrogated inside. What was it all about? He doubted whether the Inspector had all the facts. And he did not reckon he would ever get them. Perhaps his uncle might know. He would ask him later.

II

Restoration work on the Abbey was in progress. Several gangs of men, two and three strong, were working on the walls from short scaffolding runs, replacing the perished mortar in the stone walls. Many of the visitors, loaded down with bags, cameras, and recalcitrant offspring, found the sight of craftsmen at work of far more interest than the ancient pile itself.

Talebov entered the Abbey through the north transept, turned past the Lady Chapel, circled the altar, ambled through the crowds into Saint Michael's Chapel, and exited through the south transept. He walked round the grounds then returned to the paddock where he had parked his car.

The woman was the first to join him. She was dressed in jeans and a crew-neck sweater. The two men, both sporting cameras, were not far behind. 'Glad you could make it,' said Talebov. He started the engine and drove off.

He drove through Leiston and took the Aldringham road. 'The house is up ahead,' he explained. 'Keys are in the glove compartment, Yuri,' he said to the man in the passenger seat. 'The other keys are for the green microbus in the garage.' Yuri retrieved the keys.

On the other side of Aldringham, on the outskirts of Aldeburgh, he turned left into Warren Hill Lane, and parked at the first gateway. 'I haven't been inside, yet, but Whiston said he had stocked it up. Okay?' The two men and the woman got out. 'I'll see you tonight.'

He reversed onto the main road and went back the way he had just come until he came to the telephone box. He dialled the number Whiston had given him. It was not Whiston who answered, but the *parole* was correct for the day. What he heard confirmed his suspicions. There was a hidden hand at work.

III

He approached the *River Queen* cautiously on foot, having parked the car in Alde Lane and tramped across King's Field and round to the mooring at Brick Dock. There were plenty of people around, but none of them paid him any attention. The old fisherman sat outside the clapperboard hut.

'Any callers?' asked Talebov.

He took his pipe from his mouth, exposing his gums. 'No, sir, Mr Buckner. Nobody at all.'

'They must have been delayed,' said Talebov.

'Could well have been. Traffic's bad this time of the year. Mr Penfield was up asking why you weren't berthed at Pettit's dock?'

'Was he? I'll speak to him later.'

Talebov gave him a couple of pounds. 'Thanks anyway.'

'What should I do with this?' asked the fisherman. He produced the slip of paper which Talebov had given him.

Talebov took out a pen. 'Here,' he said. The man

handed over the paper. Talebov crossed out the phone number of the Wentworth Hotel. 'I'm going to play golf up at Thorpeness,' he lied, writing down the telephone number of the clubhouse. 'I'll be there until late evening.'

'Right you are,' he said, and tucked the note away in the pocket of his grimy cardigan. 'Be seeing you.'

The police had been to Penfield's house. That was what he had heard from Whiston's colleague. But no visitors at the boat yet. Unless the fisherman was lying. He climbed on board the boat and unlocked the hatch. There was nothing incriminating for anybody to find. The golf clubs were in the boot of the car and that was fitted with a wailing, anti-thief device.

He knew he would have to use the boat up until the last minute before the grab to prevent any precipitate action by those who he knew now had him under long-range surveillance. Talebov stretched out on the bunk, and closed his eyes, a faint smile on his lips. He hoped all attention would be kept on the *River Queen*.

IV

'I think it was '73 when I was last here,' said Maitland. 'With Mother and Simon. Just the three of us for the last week of the Festival.'

'But why is it called the Aldeburgh Festival when most of the major events take place at Snape?' asked Julia. They were walking arm in arm down the High Street.

'You've heard of Benjamin Britten, haven't you?' said Maitland.

'Of course,' said Julia. 'And Peter Pears.'

'Well, they founded the Festival here, in Aldeburgh, in

1948. They hoped that it would become the centre for Music and the Arts in East Suffolk. And so it has. But, it grew so popular that it was decided to build a permanent Festival site. And the one at Snape Maltings was chosen.'

'And that's where the concert hall and the opera house are?'

'Yes. But all round this area, during Festival fortnight, in halls, churches, cinemas, anywhere in fact, there'll be concerts and choirs, you name it, all connected with the Festival.'

'I see,' said Julia, 'And . . . Hang on.' She tugged Maitland's arm. 'This must be it.' They stopped outside an ironmongers.

'Are you sure?' asked Maitland.

'It's what the receptionist at the hotel told me.'

They went inside. The shop smelt of paraffin and carbolic soap. The woman behind the counter had a large supply of footmaps of the immediate vicinity. Maitland paid for a map of the Aldeburgh area.

'How about some lunch?' suggested Julia as they left the shop.

'There's a pub just down the road. I'll just have time for a pint and a quick bite before reporting to Victoria Road.'

Inside the pub, Maitland ordered the drinks and food while Julia opened the map on the table. 'Snape is only about six miles away,' she reported to Maitland when he returned with the tray of drinks. 'We could walk over there in the morning.'

Maitland looked over her shoulder. 'And there's Leiston, too. About the same distance. I think there's an Abbey up there.'

'Yes, there is,' said Julia. 'And what's this?' She pointed. 'The House in the Clouds. Doesn't that sound strange?

We'll have to go and see that. It's not all that far from Leiston. And Sizewell is just there on the coast.'

V

Nike brought a chair for Dewhurst.

'Where's Maitland?'

'At the hotel. He said he would be over after lunch,' said Nike.

'Keep him downstairs. I don't want him up here prying.'

'Don't worry,' said Capstick. 'He hasn't shown that much interest. When he was in yesterday, he just mooched around in one of the rooms, had a chat, then left.'

'He's only to be alerted after *Juniper* is operational and the road blocks are set up.' Dewhurst waited for confirmation from his two subordinates before continuing. 'Right. What have we so far?'

The room they were in was the smallest of the five bedrooms. The only furniture was the three chairs, a rickety table and Nike's single divan bed. A heavy white blanket over the rectangular window acted as curtains.

'So far,' began Capstick, 'we've only spotted Talebov.'

'And he's GRU,' interrupted Dewhurst sharply.

'Is that important?' asked Capstick.

'Zarev's KGB. Dingle is tied in with them, too. I would have expected KGB people to be involved in getting Zarev out.'

'But Talebov could be KGB now. We've no record on him after 1979. Nor have the CIA. Langley confirmed last night,' said Capstick. 'He might have swopped uniforms.'

'Unlikely,' said Dewhurst. He took off his glasses and

177

glanced round for something to clean them on. Nike produced a gleaming white handkerchief for him. 'Thanks. Of course,' he continued. 'The KGB could be in the doghouse over the *Cedar* affair, and the GRU could have been brought in to show the KGB how it should be done.'

'Seems reasonable,' said Capstick.

Dewhurst gave him a stoney glare. Capstick always searched for the easy way out. He never recognized, never mind confronted, a problem unless it hit him square on the jaw. Dewhurst disliked him intensely. But he needed him for this job. 'Reasonable,' he reiterated. 'But not necessarily correct.' He polished the lenses thoroughly and returned the glasses to their perch. 'So. At the moment, Talebov is alone?'

'Yes. But he won't be acting alone.'

'I know. I know,' replied Dewhurst impatiently. 'But where he goes, the others will follow. Map?'

Nike spread it on the table and smoothed it flat.

It was sheet 156 of the Ordnance Survey Land Ranger series, 1 to 50,000 scale, detailing the triangular spread of Saxmundham, Leiston and Aldeburgh.

'The *Free Zone*,' said Dewhurst pointing at the triangle which had been shaded green. 'I don't want any of your people in there,' he said to Capstick. 'No police. No SAS. No one. Not until the Russians grab Zarev. Until then, Talebov has complete freedom of movement. Now where's the boat? What's it called?'

'The *River Queen*,' said Capstick leaning forward. With an orange felt-tipped pen, he drew a big circle around Aldeburgh, followed by another, smaller one inside the first. 'The boat's there at Brick Dock. And we're here, about half a mile away. Victoria Road. You can see the dock from our window.' He stabbed at the map with the pen tip.

Dewhurst went across to the window and pulled back the curtain. On his left he saw a wooded expanse. Straight ahead, across the open fields criss-crossed with tracks, he saw the River Alde.

'Brick Dock's on the right,' said Capstick.

Dewhurst came back to the table. 'Okay. The Russians lift Zarev in Saxmundham and then make for the boat. As soon as that happens, the SAS move in.'

'Yes,' replied Capstick. 'One squad will invest the *River Queen*, and the other two will take up positions in and around the dock. They've been instructed to take Zarev and at least one of the Russians alive.'

Dewhurst inspected the map again. 'Talebov and his team can come into Aldeburgh either by the coast road or the main Saxmundham road.'

'And as soon as the Russians are at the dock, the whole area behind them will be sealed off. They'll have nowhere to go,' said Capstick.

Dewhurst traced the River Alde with his index finger. 'And if they make it to the boat and board her?'

'It's quite a long stretch of river,' said Capstick. 'From Aldeburgh to Slaughden, Orford and finally down to the North Sea at Shingle Street. If they manage to break out down the river, the SAS have a team just north of Orford. There's a military complex there, and the SAS can blockade the river within a matter of minutes with the help of the Army.'

Dewhurst nodded his head, satisfied. 'Nike?' He held out his hand. Nike produced an AA map of the area, showing the whole stretch of the East Suffolk countryside and coastline. 'Beyond the *Free Zone*,' said Dewhurst, 'we have a three mile *Neutral Zone*. And beyond that, the SAS roadblocks of the *Ring of Steel*.' Dewhurst shoved the map across to Capstick. 'So Talebov has plenty of room to breathe and we will have plenty of time to see which way he jumps.'

'Will all this be necessary? After all, Talebov has only one means of escape.'

'He also has a very fast car. And there is a fleet of East German trawlers working the North Sea. Outside territorial waters, but within a couple of hours' sailing time of Great Yarmouth.'

Capstick frowned. 'He wouldn't take . . .'

'One of the trawlers has asked permission to call at Great Yarmouth for some repairs. The request is being considered. Talebov obviously has a back-up escape route in case anything happens to his plans with the *River Queen*.'

'I see,' said Capstick. 'He could use his own boat or the trawler to get to the submarine.'

'Yes,' said Dewhurst. 'The submarine will be submerged beneath the trawlers using them as a screen to avoid detection. So the SAS roadblocks are essential in case he takes off for Yarmouth. Either way, he will be contained. No matter which way he moves, as soon as he leaves the *Free Zone* all the roads, all possible escape routes, will be covered.'

'Well that's it,' said Capstick.

'Has Zarev been fitted with bleepers?' asked Dewhurst.

Capstick nodded. 'In the heels of his shoes. We activate them every time he leaves the house.'

'Does he know about them?'

'No.'

'Good. What about communications?'

'We've a land-line direct to the observation post in the house above Zarev's house. And we're linked in with Neatis Head, GCHQ and the London Centre. The big bedroom at the top of the stairs is the communications room. The SAS are also tied in to us. Their command post is at the local life-boat station, just down the road.'

'Good,' said Dewhurst. His voice was confident. 'All we have to do now is wait for Mr Talebov to make the first move.'

VI

Yuri drew the curtains closed as darkness descended in the room. He switched on all the lights before resuming his seat next to Talebov.

'You will be in the bus, Leonid,' said Talebov. 'Yuri. You will come with me in the car. We will leave it at the railway station then go on foot. I will come up the hill behind him, you'll come down hill from the direction of the house. As we close in on him, Leonid, you bring up the micro-bus. Nice and quietly. No squealing brakes and revving engine. Okay?' The two men nodded. 'Then we just take him away.'

The woman entered the room. 'Everything's set. Whiston reports that the trawler should be in Yarmouth by early evening. And he made the full payment this afternoon to Battersea. Eight-thirty at Snape.'

'Thank you, Nadia,' said Talebov. His soldier's instincts had warned of a hidden hand. Now all his measures had been put into effect to counter it.

Moscow, Russia

'It was a routine raid on the Zaradye cinema. It is a known haunt of these deviants.' The Militia captain let his disgust show through in his words.

'Thank you, captain,' said General Chebrikov. He was mortified. The Militia had made the arrest, and charged Vadim. He couldn't stop the court case now. If it had been an indiscretion with a woman, yes. But not with another man. He wouldn't interfere. To do so would tarnish him; he'd be tarred with the same brush, once the rumours started.

The captain produced a sheaf of hand-written papers. 'He wrote this out himself in the cell. He asked that it be given to you personally. I haven't read it.'

Chebrikov took the papers. 'You will not allow Vadim to communicate with me again.'

'Understood, Comrade General.' He saluted. 'Will that be all?'

'Yes.' The captain made a swift exit. Chebrikov began to read.

The letter detailed how Vadim had given way, after years of indecision, to the unnatural urges that had tormented him. He apologized for any embarrassment his arrest would cause the General. He then spoke of how he had been led in to a homosexual trap by the GRU and how they, or rather General Lyalin, had forced him to spy on his superior.

Vadim's confession rambled on and on, and Chebrikov read it over and over. When he had finally digested it, he left his office and drove across to the Kremlin. First he contacted Fedorchuk. Then both men went in search of the Premier.

Snape, England

I

'Delicious,' said Julia, and licked the cream from her finger-tips. But she was unaware of the white moustache just below her nose.

'Here,' said Maitland with affection. He leaned across the table and dabbed her mouth with his napkin. 'Take it easy,' he admonished as she packed her mouth with the remainder of the cream slice, like a child at a tea-party, eager to be gone to play but determined to have its fill. 'We've got plenty of time.'

Julia gulped and emptied her mouth. 'But I want to visit the Marland Gallery before we go. And I want to browse through the Festival Marquee too. There's lots to see,' she added, the enthusiasm in her voice matching her animated features. She finished her coffee and picked up the Festival handbook. 'And then there's . . .'

'Okay. Okay. But there's no hurry.' Maitland checked his watch. 'If we get a taxi about five-thirty back to Alde-burgh, that'll leave us plenty of time to brush-up, change and be back here for the concert.'

They had left Aldeburgh on foot after breakfast armed with the map they had bought the previous day. Julia was intent on seeing as much of the area as their short stay would allow. It was a beautifully warm summer's day, one of those days that are forever tucked away in everybody's memories and which can readily be evoked by the redolence of swaying blooms and the smell of new-mown grass. The flat, verdant, Suffolk countryside looked as if it had just been freshly painted, and the sun, high in the clear blue sky, twinkled and danced its rays over the slow-moving River Alde.

At Blackheath Corner, they had stopped for a rest and had consulted the map. The road divided into two. Maitland had wanted to go right, to Leiston, to spend some time at the Abbey. But Julia had plumped for continuing straight ahead, to Snape and the Maltings complex, promising Maitland that they would go to Leiston Abbey the following morning.

'I'm ready,' said Julia.

Maitland finished his coffee and stood up. 'Right. The Marland Gallery. That's, er ...' He glanced left, then right. 'Over that way, I think,' he added as he pointed. He frowned. 'Over there. Look. Isn't that Simon?'

Julia turned in the direction he was pointing. 'Where? Oh, yes. I see him. It is Simon.'

'I wonder what he's doing here?'

II

They sat in Simon's car in the car park, uncle and nephew. In the rear-view mirror, Maitland could see Julia waiting impatiently by the barrier, casting dark looks in their direction, uncertain as to what was going on, concerned by the abrupt arrival of Simon, and the equally unexpected hijacking of her fiancé.

Maitland used the sight of Julia as a beacon, as a constant beam that shone through the cloying dust and dirt, the clouds and smog, that arose to envelop him as his world and all he believed in collapsed about his ears.

III

The official with the blue badge directed Nadia towards the Festival Marquee. 'They have a stall inside,' he told her.

Nadia thanked him and went inside. She had difficulty finding the Air Hanson booth as it was hidden behind another away from the main thoroughfares which were crowded with meandering visitors. When she did eventually locate it, the girl was not there, and a scrawled note informed Nadia that she would be back in ten minutes.

Nadia wandered off among the aisles until she saw the Air Hanson stewardess return to take up duty again at the booth. Nadia went over and introduced herself.

'Good afternoon,' said Nadia. 'I am Mrs Euler.'

'Oh, yes. I've been expecting you,' replied the stewardess. 'My name is Anthea.'

They chatted together for a couple of minutes then Anthea took Nadia outside. 'This way,' said Anthea and led Nadia along a path which crossed the entrance to the Concert Hall restaurant. 'It's not far,' she said as they climbed a hillock and took the track that wound across a wide expanse of long grass. The River Alde gurgled past on their left.

'It will come in here,' said Anthea. The tall grass had given way to a large square of black, bare earth in which a white circle had been marked out. 'So you can see there's not much of a walk from the Hall. But Mrs Euler, I would be grateful if you could arrange to have everybody here by twenty-fifteen for a quick briefing. We run a very tight schedule on the Snape shuttle.'

'I will try,' said Nadia.

Anthea took out some brochures from her pocket. 'And could you distribute these among the group. Just a few safety rules and precautions for them.'

Aldeburgh, England

I

They drove back to the hotel in a despairing silence. The taxi-driver had tried to pass the time of day with them but had given up when his efforts had been met by a mournful silence.

Maitland sat to one side, his eyes blank, his mouth clamped shut, his clenched fists slowly grinding into his knees. Whenever Julia tried to touch him, he shrank deeper into the corner, his gesture maintaining the distance between them, a no-man's land she was forbidden to enter. She pleaded in whispers to him but he made no response, and, when they arrived at the Wentworth, he got out without a word, leaving her to pay off the cab.

He shambled into the hotel like an old man, and went straight up to their room. When Julia arrived, he was locked in the toilet.

'Ollie,' she cried. 'What's the matter? Please tell me. Please let me in.'

Maitland sat on the toilet seat, tears in his eyes, oblivious to the calls of the distraught Julia. He was looking back into himself, searching faces and names: Dewhurst, Simon, MacKenzie, Jimmy-Jack. They paraded through his collapsed world, spectres haunting the dilapidation, signposts on the way to his own destruction.

'Simon,' he whispered tearfully to himself. 'How could you? How could you do it? Why did . . .?'

II

'I don't want you to speak. I want you to listen,' pleaded Simon. He switched on the car-radio, turning the volume down low, so that the music hummed in the background. 'Promise me you won't interrupt. It's dreadfully important.'

Maitland was bemused. 'I promise, if that's what you want,' he replied. This was not the Simon he knew: he was as pale as his white hair which was tousled, and his hands shook uncontrollably.

'What I have to tell you is very important and you must act on it immediately,' said Simon. 'How I came to know what I know must be left to later. It is only of secondary importance. Do you understand?'

'I think so, Simon. But . . .'

Simon stared at his nephew. 'You know a man named Todor Zarev. He is living in Saxmundham, not far from here.'

'Zarev?' said Maitland. He was confused. Not only by his uncle's knowledge, but by the fact that he himself had forgotten about Zarev. He had assisted in the man's relocation to Saxmundham, but it had slipped his memory. For a moment he had the mistaken notion that his uncle had been involved in Zarev's move to Suffolk. 'Sorry, Simon. But Zarev? How do you . . .?' He shook his head.

Simon held up his hands. They were trembling. 'You promised, Ollie. Let me finish. It is very difficult for me.'

'What are you saying, Simon? How do you know about Zarev?' he groaned.

Simon squeezed Maitland's hand. 'You must hear me out about Zarev,' he implored. 'Zarev has been used as bait to lure four Russian agents into this country.'

'Oh Simon,' said Maitland weakly.

'Your people, MI5, hope to capture the Russians and use their presence here to demonstrate to Britain and the world not only hostile Soviet intentions, but also Soviet duplicity and insincerity in the Kremlin's desire for peaceful coexistence and nuclear disarmament.'

'Simon. Please. How do you know all this? Please tell me,' said Maitland.

'Because I am a Soviet agent myself,' said Simon quickly. 'I have been for almost forty years.'

III

Julia tapped on the door again. 'Ollie. Ollie. Please let me in,' she said.

Maitland sat upright and covered his ears. He needed time to think and reassess. He had to regress stage by stage, impression by impression, through the last six years of his life. Because he was the key to it all. Dewhurst and MacKenzie had arranged it that way. He had been alternately sheltered and exposed by them, pushed out from the centre by layers of lies and deceit, until he stood alone, naked, waiting for the final act that had been skilfully built and orchestrated all around him.

And then there was Simon. The wild card. Simon who had come to warn him. Simon the traitor.

IV

'I wasn't a spy as such,' said Simon. His left hand rested on the gear lever. 'What you would call a talent-spotter. I pointed the KGB in the direction of bright young men and women at Oxford who, like me, were disillusioned and disenchanted with the system. That was all.'

'That was all?' exclaimed Maitland. 'A traitor to your country. And to me. To everything.' Tears rolled down his cheeks. He swallowed back his emotions and his voice became ladened with sarcasm. 'No you weren't a traitor. Sorry, Simon. You just suborned others into becoming traitors. Your hands are clean.' He leaned across his uncle. 'And you say that was all?' he prodded Simon in the chest.

'You have no right to be angry, Ollie. Certainly not at me. I experienced the fabrications, the intrigues and the propaganda during the war. I hoped that peace would bring change. But it didn't. The scheming and plotting continued unabated. We just shifted our focus from Germany to Russia, to Poland, to Albania. The same battle was still in progress. Democracy versus Totalitarianism.' Simon laughed lightly. 'We in Britain have a democracy. But it is merely a list of platitudes. Beneath the surface, in the world you now inhabit, Ollie, there is a hard core of murderous mendacity. That is why I left the Service in 1951.'

'But not in Russia, eh?' snapped Maitland. He had a mental image of Dewhurst and MacKenzie; he saw them as one. In the background loomed the visage of Gouzenko, blurred and indistinct, but melting into the composite features of the other two.

'Paranoia and distrust underlie the activities of the Soviets, just as they did throughout the reign of the Imperial Court. That is the nature of the beast, caught on the crossroads between Europe and Asia for centuries, never sure of which way to turn, which flank to defend. As a result, the Russians have habitually indulged in espionage and destabilization; it is part and parcel of their make-up. But if we choose to meet and confront them on their terms, using their methods, then we betray the essence of our own beliefs. We become, in the eyes of the Russians, and the pawn countries we manipulate, no better than the Russians. Worse in fact, because the gap between our worlds, our well-advertised, superior moral stance, and the deeds we perpetrate, becomes cavernous.'

Maitland suddenly realized that Simon had stopped talking. His thoughts were in turmoil. He struggled to find a rejoinder. 'You are a traitor. You have betrayed this country,' was all he could think to say.

'This country had been betrayed and sold out long before I came on the scene. Betrayed by the very men, the politicians, whom the people had mandated to govern them. The politicians have abdicated their responsibility, have allowed MI5 and MI6 an independent life, an existence above and beyond all democratic constraints. These security agencies now rule and they have nothing but scorn and contempt for the democratic institutions of this land and its inhabitants. The Russians know this and their distrust of us will never end. Why should it? All they can see is a beast very similar to themselves. There is no need, no impetus, for change, for trust. Our example is sufficient to maintain the Soviets in their historical paranoia. The Cold War and the arms race will never cease until we can convince the Russians that we are different.'

'I trust you will leave your thoughts to posterity. You will have plenty of spare time to jot them down,' said Maitland bitterly. 'In prison.'

'I had to make a choice,' continued Simon. 'I could not sit back, listening to the prevarications and witnessing the distortions, without doing something. By doing nothing, I was giving implicit consent to all that was happening. I made a responsible decision, I believe. I elected to work for the Russians. Had I not done so, my life would have been a meaningless sham.'

'You are a sham, Simon.'

Simon touched his nephew on the shoulder. He turned away. 'Ollie, I once said to you that you have first to identify the enemy before you can decide what to defend. I found my enemy in the corridors of Whitehall and Westminster. I chose to fight them in order to defend my country.'

'Just words. Meaningless words,' said Maitland. He buried his face in his hands. 'Thank god mother is no longer alive. No wonder you kept her in the dark about your work for MI5.'

'Perhaps. But she knew of my work for the Russians. She didn't approve. But she hated your father; she never showed that to you. I was working against him and his ilk. She was happy about that.'

V

Maitland opened the toilet door. Julia flew into his arms. She kissed him wildly, on the cheek, on the nose, the lips and the forehead. He could feel the wetness of her tears.

'Darling. Darling, what is it? Tell me,' she mumbled as they kissed.

Maitland broke her embrace. He held her by the wrists. 'I will tell you very shortly. Not now,' he added, as he saw her expectant look. 'Later. When I get back.'

'Where are you going? Don't leave me. There's something awfully wrong, isn't there. I'm afraid.' She pressed herself against him.

He stared at her. His life, he had concluded, had been a complete and utter sham. From the beginning, he had had no control: others, his father, Simon, yes, even his mother, had each woven their webs of deception around him. But later, at MI5, with Dewhurst and MacKenzie, he had allowed them to create and conjure up their perversions, while he had stood idly by. He hadn't lived his own life; had never made a decision that was his own, that had not been, in one way or the other, a product of someone else's machination. But now he was about to.

'I'll be gone an hour. I want you to get packed and be waiting for me downstairs when I return. Then we're going away. Out of this godforsaken country.'

'Ollie . . .'

'Do as I ask, please Julia. I have to go.' He kissed her quickly on the cheek, collected the car keys and went downstairs.

Simon was waiting for him at reception.

Saxmundham, England

I

Nike had put his team on alert. Dewhurst had told him that the Russians would make their move that evening or the following one.

He had been down to the cellar to check out the *Semtex* and the detonating mechanisms in the pouches, and to ensure his men had completed their inventory of equipment and weapons. Everything was as it should be.

He went upstairs to the top of the house. The two watchers on duty were at the window. Nike joined them. He looked over their shoulders, picked out Zarev's house, the approach roads and possible escape routes, and glanced across the rooftops of the town over the fields in the direction of Leiston and the Sizewell plant. He grinned to himself in anticipation.

It all fitted so neatly. As Mr Dewhurst had planned. Nike went over to the coffee machine and poured himself a cup without offering to do so for his two companions. He noted the exchange of looks between the two men but he ignored them.

Fuck them, he thought. They were just office dross. Their job would soon be over. And then his would begin. He sensed a tingling at his extremities, and a desire to get on with his work. But he would have to be patient. He would be pulling the trigger.

As soon as Zarev was snatched, then his team of

erstwhile saboteurs would go into action. Under cover of darkness they would cut their way into the Sizewell installation and leave a series of incriminating trails and evidence of *Spetsnaz* intrusion. Then they would retreat.

Meanwhile the Russians would have been apprehended. Then Inspector Curtiss, in charge of security at the plant, would be informed and told to sit tight until a bomb disposal squad arrived. A security blanket would be thrown over the whole area. The bomb squad, Nike's four-man team, would then smuggle in the explosive and place it at the prearranged locations, while Curtiss and his men scoured the perimeter fence for signs of entry, uncovering as they did so, the evidence of Russian intrusion. Then the *Semtex* would be discovered, disarmed and then removed with Curtiss as witness, and the brave bomb-disposal men would leave to a chorus of grateful regards.

Nike thought it was all too wonderful. Later, news would begin to leak out about what had happened. Selected local inhabitants would talk to tame journalists; the Home Office would hint, then deny; one or two members of Parliament of the right political persuasion would raise the matter in the House. And so on, thought Nike. It could not fail. No one would mention, in an official capacity that is, the casualties suffered by the security forces in the arrest of the Russian saboteurs. Nobody would question the death of Oliver Maitland. Not even the vacillating MacKenzie. His death would be a regrettable sacrifice in the fight against Soviet subversion. At least that is what the Security Service would say.

II

Maitland had insisted they use his car when Simon demanded to accompany him. Now they were only a couple of miles from Saxmundham but for some reason the urgency of the situation had not transmitted itself to that part of Maitland's brain that controlled his driving. He idled along at under thirty miles an hour, as if he were out for a casual evening drive through the countryside.

He kept glancing across at his uncle as if to confirm that it was indeed Simon sitting next to him and not the product of an aberrant imagination. Maitland had finally accepted the fact that this man, a man whom he had known and loved all his life, the uncle that had been both father and brother, a friend whose shoulder he had often borrowed, was a despicable traitor and deceiver of the highest, or rather, the lowest, order. He expected Simon to change before his eyes, his nose to grow long and pointed, his hair to change colour to black, his lips to become thin and shrew-like. The changes would then correspond with the connotations his mind had juggled with in coming to terms with his uncle's treachery.

Simon had changed, the mask had slipped, but no physical transformation had been wrought. The changes had occurred inside, many years ago. And now Maitland could feel himself change. Perhaps his own features had been altered by his uncle's confession. He glimpsed himself in the mirror. They hadn't. But then . . .

'Why did the Russians ask you to contact me?' Maitland suddenly blurted out.

'Because they know we are related,' said Simon. 'They thought it would be the quickest and best way, given the circumstances and the gravity of the situation.'

Maitland frowned. 'I don't understand how . . .'

'Besides, the whole operation had Dewhurst's name written all over it,' added Simon.

'I thought as much,' said Maitland. 'You've read the contents of that package I asked you to hold for me.'

'Yes.'

'And of course the KGB know of it, too.'

'It wasn't particularly bright of you to ask me to keep it for you, was it?'

'I didn't know you were a spy then,' said Maitland scornfully.

'I mean that Dewhurst has had me under surveillance for some time now. He's probably guessed I have a copy. It wouldn't take his heavies a great deal of time and effort to extract its hiding place from me.'

Maitland shuddered. How stupid he had been. Nike would have made mincemeat out of Simon. Stupid man that I am, he thought. Fool. Idiot. He did not understand what it was all about. He was still a novice in a world of studied, calculated evil and intrigue.

'I never tried to use your affection for me to influence you, Ollie,' said Simon, as if the thought had just occurred to him.

'You never tried to talent spot me, you mean. But you have always tried to influence me. All those talks and chats about . . .'

'That would have been the same had I not been what I was, had you not been a serving officer in MI5. I am your uncle first and foremost.'

'You just wanted me to have a good, all-round view of things, eh?'

'Yes. That is true. I did not want you growing up as short-sighted and narrow-minded as your father. Your mother wanted it that way. We hoped you'd learn to think for yourself.'

'I am doing. Finally. Don't you worry about that.' He had come to a decision. A neutral one. He wouldn't help the Russians to extricate themselves from the trap. But he wouldn't help MI5 to close in on them by remaining inactive. He chose, instead, to remove the honey-pot. He would take Zarev out of the middle, if it wasn't too late, in the hope that the Russians would abort their mission when they found he was not there. Then he would contact Dewhurst and MacKenzie and tell them what he had done, and make them pull back their troops. If they refused, he would threaten them not only with the details of the Zarev ploy being made public, but he would resurrect and have published the evidence he had linking Dewhurst with the murder at Mullaghmore.

'What are you thinking?' asked Simon.

'About my useless life.' Stupid life is what he felt he should have said.

'You're making amends now,' said his uncle, and he patted Maitland's knee.

Maitland's voice had lost its belligerent tone. 'I doubt it,' he confessed. 'It's probably too late.'

'But you are going to try?'

'Yes,' said Maitland. 'For both our sakes, Simon.' It was the first time he had called him Simon since that afternoon. For some reason, Maitland felt relieved.

'We're almost there,' warned Simon. 'Do you know the way?'

'Yes,' Maitland manoeuvred the car into the right-hand lane and waited for the lights to change.

He turned into the town centre, crossed the level-crossing and turned right at the public house.

III

Talebov left his BMW in the station car park and walked up the hill. He noted the tall tower seemingly perched atop the roofs of the houses in the distance. Up ahead, turning right by the pub, he saw the waddling figure of Zarev, a brown Homburg fitted tightly to the bald pate.

The town was relatively quiet and there were few pedestrians on the streets. It suited Talebov admirably. Fewer witnesses would mean less possible interference, less cause for alarm, less need to share suspicion with the police.

But it was not that which really bothered him. It was the lurking presence of the hidden hand. He sensed a trap. But he was prepared. The Uzi, buried under his armpit beneath his windcheater, gave him security. He would use it if he had to.

He caught up with Zarev as he neared the fire-station. A car passed him, slowly edging up the hill, its two passengers, one young, one old, intent on the road ahead. In the distance Talebov could see Yuri walking towards him down the hill, while Leonid was also in position, behind the wheel of the micro-bus.

Snape, England

The crowds, the myriad accents, the summer excitement, had subsided as the concert-goers had taken their seats for the evening performance. Small gaggles of tourists and sight-seers wandered over the complex, and Nadia was glad of the respite from the earlier hustle and bustle. Anthea was waiting.

'Ah, Mrs Euler. The flight will be in shortly,' she said, pointing at a black dot in the sky.

'Good,' said Nadia. She swung her bag over her shoulder. The butt of the Uzi struck her spine.

'And the rest of the party?' asked Anthea.

'They will be here shortly. I did pass on all your instructions.'

'Well, I hope they arrive soon. The pilot will not want to be kept waiting. He has his schedule to maintain.'

'I'm sure they will,' replied Nadia with confidence. She walked a few yards away from the Air Hanson hostess who was frowning with worry. 'We won't keep the pilot waiting,' she added archly.

'Here it comes,' announced Anthea. She looked back to the main complex. 'I don't see the rest of your party, Mrs Euler.'

The last of her words were drowned in the shuddering beat of the helicopter's rotors. Anthea held on to her hat as the downdraught swept across the field.

The aircraft landed in the clearing, and the surrounding grass bent and swayed in the artificial wind. 'Don't approach the aircraft, Mrs Euler, until I tell you,' said Anthea.

Nadia gave her a vacant smile, nodded, and proceeded towards the helicopter.

'Mrs Euler,' cried Anthea. 'Come back. What about the rest of your friends?' She set off in pursuit of the bogus Mrs Euler.

As she neared the aircraft, Nadia could see the pilot signalling for her to get back. Nadia kept on. She reached the passenger door a few strides ahead of the running Anthea. She pulled back the safety catch, slid open the door, and levered herself inside.

Anthea followed. Nadia gave her a helping hand up inside the cabin.

'What are you doing, Mrs Euler?' demanded Anthea, casting a frightened glance at the pilot who was on his feet, glaring sternly at the two women.

In reply Nadia punched Anthea on the nose. The hostess collapsed to the floor. The pilot's mouth gaped open in astonishment. Before he had a chance to react, Nadia stretched out and pulled the earphones from his head, then struck him viciously in the mouth with the back of her hand.

The man was dazed, both by what he had seen and the blow Nadia had so savagely delivered. She grabbed him by the throat and dragged him from the cockpit. He stumbled and fell, tripping over the prostrate form of Anthea.

Nadia took the Uzi out of her bag and knelt before the pilot. He sat up on one elbow and ran a hand across his bloody lips. 'I can fly this machine,' she told him, prodding him in the chest with the muzzle of the gun. 'I don't need you. So I won't think twice about killing you, or her, if you don't do exactly what I say. Understand?'

'Yes,' whispered the pilot.

Nadia stood up and backed away. 'Close the door. Then

strap her in. No heroics or we may all wind up dead.' She stood to one side while the pilot went about his tasks. When he had finished, Nadia continued. 'Did you have full tanks when you left Battersea?'

The pilot nodded. 'Yes. Regulations,' he stammered.

'Good.' Nadia was happy. There would be sufficient fuel to take the helicopter more than two hundred miles, out to the rendezvous with the fishing fleet and the submarine in the North Sea. 'Now get back to the cockpit. I will tell you where to fly this machine.'

Saxmundham, England

I

'That's him,' exclaimed Maitland. He slowed the car to a stop. 'Zarev. On the other side of the road.'

'Are you sure?' asked Simon, leaning across his nephew.

'Yes.' He applied the hand-brake, unlatched his seat belt and got out of the car. He ran across the road. Zarev was passing the articulated gates of the fire station.

At first, Zarev appeared not to have noticed Maitland's approach. He was walking with his head bent forward as if he were studying the passage of his feet over the grey pavement. When he finally heard Maitland's footsteps, he stopped and looked furtively around, his movements resembling those of an animal suddenly aware of imminent danger.

Maitland reached in his pocket for his identification card. Zarev misinterpreted the gesture and threw up his hands to shield his face, while at the same time, he backed himself up against the wall of the station, emitting a strangled, keening whimper.

'Mr Zarev,' said Maitland. He parted the man's hands with his card. 'Mr Dewhurst sent me,' he lied. Maitland had expected such a reaction from Zarev, knowing that he lived in fear of reprisal from the KGB. He had decided to go softly with Zarev, and lie if necessary, in order to impress him with his authority and not to spook him. 'Would you come with me, please.'

Zarev cowered against the wall. He gripped Maitland's wrist with both hands and pushed it away from his face to inspect the identification card.

'Come with me,' repeated Maitland, as he saw Zarev visibly relax. He took the man by the elbow and gently guided him across the road.

II

'This is it!' shouted Gregson, one of the watchers at the window. He had his binoculars trained on the action below. Nike came to join him at his vantage point. Gregson handed over the glasses and pointed. 'Down by the fire station.'

Nike put the glasses to his eyes and refocused them. He scanned the unfolding drama.

'I'll turn on the bleeper,' said Gregson, and walked across to the control panel.

'Fuck me!' exploded Nike. 'What the hell is Maitland doing there with Zarev?'

III

Talebov saw the car stop, a man get out and run over to Zarev. What the hell was going on? He didn't wait for his mind to permutate the possibilities; he reacted with his soldier's instincts, running forward, unzipping his wind-cheater and pulling free the Uzi. He saw Yuri break into a trot, and he heard the coughing splutter of the micro-bus starting up.

He reached the car at the same time as Zarev and the tall man. Zarev saw him first: he clung on to Maitland and began to bleat. Maitland was thrown off balance and as he turned, Talebov shoved the Uzi under his chin, forcing his head back. The bus drew up alongside, coinciding with Yuri's arrival.

'You, in the car,' said Talebov. 'Stay still. Get Zarev in the bus.' He nodded at Leonid. Yuri had drawn his weapon and he used it to coax Zarev away from the protecting presence of Maitland. Talebov backed Maitland away from the car. He signalled Simon with his left hand. 'Move over into the driver's seat. Slowly,' he ordered. Yuri prodded Zarev into the back of the bus.

Simon did as he was told. '*Sosed. Neighbour*,' he said to Talebov who turned to face him and frowned. 'I am here on the authority of General Chebrikov, Colonel Talebov.'

Talebov pulled Maitland closer to the car. He glanced around, saw the street was still deserted, then leaned closer to Simon. 'What did you say?'

'The distance between Dzerzhinsky Square and Znamensky Street is but a short one,' said Simon, giving the recognition *parole* employed between K G B and G R U agents abroad.

'Who's this?' asked Talebov nodding at Maitland.

'Never mind for now,' said Simon. He climbed out of the car. 'Let's get off the street.'

'Into the bus,' ordered Talebov. He grabbed Maitland by the shoulder. 'Move.'

IV

Nike came flying down the stairs, his face suffused with rage. He darted into the kitchen where his men were eating supper. 'Get your guns and follow me. Now!' He roared. He dashed out into the forecourt and got into his car. He switched on the small screen below the radio console and watched the picture appear. It showed the immediate area over which a red dot was moving in the direction of Leiston. He picked up his handset and called Dewhurst in Aldeburgh.

'What's going on?' demanded Dewhurst.

'Maitland's here,' said Nike. 'And the Russians. They're all together. In a green bus heading towards Leiston.' His four men arrived and scrambled in with a great deal of clamour. 'Shut up, you noisy bastards,' cried Nike.

'What was that?' shouted Dewhurst.

Nike was panicking. 'Sorry. I wasn't talking to you.'

'I'll alert the SAS teams to man the roadblocks. You keep that bus in range. They might be headed for Yarmouth. But they might turn back on themselves and make for the boat. Don't lose them. I'll be mobile in a couple of minutes, then I'll get back to you.'

Leiston, England

I

Talebov was in the passenger seat of the bus. He had his window rolled down and he hung half in, half out of the cab, searching the sky while keeping up the conversation with Simon. 'I understand,' he said to Simon over his shoulder. 'But the critical phase of the operation has been reached. Abortion and completion at this stage are one and the same thing.'

Simon sat next to Maitland in the back of the bus, opposite Yuri and Zarev who was curled up in a ball behind the driver's seat. Yuri's gun sloped diagonally in the space between them, steely-blue, threatening and insolent. Simon patted Maitland's knee as he spoke. 'Will you take Zarev with you?'

'Yes,' replied Talebov, and leaned out of the window again.

Zarev began to moan as the van sped along the country road, the high hedges on either side a blur of greens and browns, shielding the view of the flat pastureland. Maitland shifted his position and tried to get a look through the windscreen. He was rewarded for his effort by a blow to the midriff from the barrel of the Uzi. He gasped loudly.

'What's going on?' said Talebov. He turned in his seat to survey the scene. 'What's he got to do with all this?' he said to Simon. The bus slowed as it came to the outskirts of Leiston. Talebov touched Leonid's elbow. 'Drive carefully,' he warned. Leonid nodded. He then pointed at Maitland again. 'What's he doing with you? Is he KGB?'

'He's MI5,' said Simon, and patted Maitland's knee again. 'He is also my nephew. My orders were to contact him for assistance.'

Talebov shook his head. 'Don't tell me any more.' He turned away, lost for words.

II

'They're in Leiston now,' said Nike. 'Hang on. They're turning. Going left. North. Probably heading for Yoxford and the main road to Yarmouth.'

'Stay with them,' warned Dewhurst. 'The SAS are ready and waiting for them. I should be in Leiston in about five minutes.'

'Should I pursue them to the roadblock?' asked Nike.

'Only until you are sure the SAS have them,' replied Dewhurst. 'Then . . .' Dewhurst paused. 'Can you hear that, Nike?'

'What? Hear what?' When no reply came, he repeated his question. 'Hear what?'

'Can you hear a helicopter?' shouted Dewhurst. 'I can see it. Coming in from the west.'

'No. No,' shrieked Nike, the panic returning.

'It must be for them. It's not the boat. Or the trawler. They're going out by helicopter.'

'Bastards,' Nike blurted out. 'Bastards.'

III

The bus turned left out of Leiston on another twisting country road. 'We're paying a visit to Leiston Abbey,' said Talebov. Leonid's response was to increase speed as if the words Talebov had spoken were a signal to complete the remainder of the journey as quickly as possible. The sudden acceleration threw Maitland against Simon and both men almost tumbled from the seats. Yuri lashed out with his weapon and caught Maitland a glancing blow on the forehead which drew blood.

'Stop it,' roared Talebov as he saw Maitland squaring up to Yuri.

Then the driver braked the bus violently and swung left-handed onto a narrow, uneven track. Everybody was rocked and thrown by the sudden manoeuvre. Maitland banged his head on the roof; Simon was thrown to his knees in front of Yuri, whose feet leapt uncontrollably in the air. He ended up on top of Zarev who had bounced forward onto the floor. Talebov was thrown against his door but he kept his Uzi trained in the direction of the mêlée in the back.

The bus slowed as it approached the car park which was half full. As the driver parked the vehicle, Talebov spoke. 'We will walk through the ruins casually like a group of visitors. Then out into the grounds where we will wait. Any trouble from either of you two,' he said glaring at Zarev then Maitland, 'and a lot of innocent tourists are going to be dead. Do as you're told and no harm will come to anybody.'

IV

Nike told his driver to stop. He examined the screen carefully.

'Well?' shouted Dewhurst.

'Give me a minute,' answered Nike angrily. Then, remembering to whom was talking, he spoke again. 'Please.' He twisted one of the knobs on the tiny console and brought the northern approach to Leiston to the centre of the monitor. 'They turned left,' he reported to Dewhurst. 'Just up ahead. And now they've stopped. But there's no left turn on the monitor's map.'

'It'll be a farm track or something, damn you,' said Dewhurst.

'Map,' said Nike to the man seated behind him. The map was pushed forward. He found the correct location. 'There's a left turn to Leiston Abbey on the map,' he reported over the radio.

'That'll be it.'

'And I can hear the helicopter,' added Nike. He opened his window and looked out. 'I can see it now.'

'Nike,' said Dewhurst. 'Get in there. The SAS are on their way. Don't let them reach that helicopter.'

V

Talebov walked in front followed by Maitland, Simon and Zarev, who were huddled together, flanked by Yuri and Leonid, two shepherds with a tiny flock of reluctant sheep.

They halted at the entrance gate while Talebov counted

out the money to the attendant. Maitland feigned interest in the commemorative plaque fixed to the gatepost while his mind juggled with the options open to him. He could try and prevent the Russians taking Zarev with them. But he would be risking not only his own life, but probably those of innocent bystanders. He could not afford to do that. He did not doubt that the Russians would open fire indiscriminately should he move against them. Also, there was always the chance that the police would become involved, and that one or more of the Russians would be captured. And that would be playing into Dewhurst's hands. No, he decided, he had to opt for inactivity. He would let the Russians take Zarev out of the country: Dewhurst's scheme would be thwarted, and he would then be left with his one and only problem, Simon.

Yuri pressed against his shoulder, breaking his thoughts, and the group passed through into the Abbey grounds, in the middle of which stood the thirteenth-century ruins. Simon stumbled on the uneven turf and Maitland lent a helping hand. Simon smiled, then arched his eyebrows as if to ask what they were doing inside the Abbey. Maitland was as much in the dark as his uncle: he had no idea why the Russians had brought them there.

The answer came almost immediately. Maitland heard the steady clatter of a helicopter and he stopped, as the others did, to peer into the sky. He was reminded of his days in Northern Ireland and the constant toing and froing of the Army's whirly birds. He located the aircraft high above a distant stand of trees, already beginning its descent towards the Abbey. Its imminent arrival was greeted with a grin from Talebov to his comrades and he urged the group forward into the Abbey.

They entered beneath the arch of the north transept and passed through the roofless nave, skirting bands of stationary tourists whose historical observations had been interrupted by the helicopter's unexpected arrival. They watched with thrown back heads and straining backs and eyes, pointing and waving, as the helicopter began to circle directly overhead. Small knots of excited children dashed hither and thither, some of them climbing to vantage points on ledges and niches cut in the reddish-brown stones, happy to be temporarily rescued from the adult chore in which they had been forced to participate.

Yuri and Leonid were now at the rear of the party and they had constantly to dodge and weave around the sight-seers to keep their flock together. Talebov, meanwhile, was striding out in front, pushing people out of the way, but they seemed not to notice this rudeness, so caught up were they in the sight of the droning aircraft up above.

They passed through the south transept and out of the Abbey into the hilly grass of the grounds again. Talebov had gone on ahead and was signalling to the helicopter pilot as he started his hovering descent. Maitland looked back the way they had just come. Yuri was immediately behind him, grinning slyly, framed in the carved stonework of the transept arch. He pushed Maitland forward, and he followed Simon and Zarev who were hugging a stretch of crumbled stonework that jutted out onto the grassland like a direction indicator, pointing the way towards the heli-copter.

As Maitland moved into the lengthening shadow cast by the wall, a new sound, urgent and deadly, made itself heard above the din of the helicopter. A volley of rapid gunfire struck the wall above Maitland's head. The whine of the ricochets sang a deathly song in the evening twilight, and chips of dislocated stone buzzed and skimmed through the air like a swarm of angry wasps. Maitland dived for-ward and grabbed his uncle by the shoulders. Both men

213

tumbled to the sweet-smelling turf in a jumble of arms and legs.

A woman screamed. Then another. Maitland wrapped a protective arm around his uncle, and raised his head a fraction. Zarev was scrabbling in the grass, trying to dig himself a hole. Talebov was on his back, extricating the Uzi from the folds of his windcheater, while his two accomplices lay face down, unmoving. Then Talebov, his weapon free, began a series of rolls that brought him back to within ten feet of Maitland. Yuri and Leonid raised their heads to indicate to Talebov that they were unhurt.

Maitland twisted his body and glanced back into the Abbey. He saw a man on his knees as if in prayer, both hands clutched to his chest which was blotted with a growing red stain. A child began to whimper, and several voices, trembling with fear, cried out in anguish.

Maitland could see several of the tourists, men and women, who moments before had been enjoying an airborne diversion, who were now frightened and scared, crawling and wriggling about within the confines of the Abbey. A woman got to her feet, only to drop to her knees again as the firing re-commenced. The bullets peppered the grass close to Maitland, coming in from two different directions, and he covered his head with his hands. There were more screams and curses and Maitland thought he heard his name called. He glanced up for a second to see Talebov slithering towards him on his stomach.

'Stay low,' hissed Talebov to the group. 'There's three of them at least.'

Maitland looked up again. There was movement inside the Abbey. Two figures darted forward towards the south transept. He recognized Nike. Maitland propped himself up on his elbows. 'Nike,' he shouted. 'Nike! What the hell are you doing? It's me, Maitland.'

Talebov pulled at his foot. 'Get down, you stupid bastard. He's shooting at you. Not at us.'

Maitland's stomach lurched as the implication of Talebov's words sank in, crystallizing the suspicions he had harboured but had suppressed throughout that afternoon.

'Yes,' he said weakly to Talebov.

The Russian turned to his two companions and spoke rapidly in his native tongue. Yuri and Leonid both nodded their understanding. Leonid began to edge forward to Zarev.

'Okay, Englishman,' said Talebov to Simon. 'When I give the word, you get up and run to the helicopter.'

'What about him?' said Simon. He pointed at Maitland.

'That's up to him. You look after yourself. Run to the helicopter. Okay?'

In the confusion, the helicopter had landed. Its wheels were barely touching the ground, and it swayed and rolled as the pilot fought to keep it ready for instantaneous take-off. As they watched, the cabin door was flung open, and a man and woman, both dressed in dark blue uniforms, leapt to the ground and scurried off towards the safety of the trees.

'Come on, Ollie,' said Simon, and he gripped his nephew's hand.

'Ready?' asked Talebov. 'Yuri and I will cover you.'

Maitland had nowhere else to go. 'Yes,' he replied.

'Then go,' roared Talebov. He got up on one knee and started shooting. Yuri returned fire also.

Maitland pulled Simon to his feet and saw that Leonid was doing the same with Zarev. All four began to run as Nike and his men returned the fire. Maitland was almost bent double trying to shield Simon from the gunfire. Bullets zig-zagged across the grass sending divots of turf flying through the air, marking out the escape route.

Simon stumbled. Maitland lost his balance and fell flat on his face. He quickly got back on his feet and reached out again for Simon, who was standing upright, exposed and vulnerable. As if in slow motion, Maitland stretched out his arms, only to see Simon move away from him, stepping backwards, his face a mask of pained surprise. Blood suddenly covered Maitland's hands and he saw Simon drift slowly to the ground, his chest a mass of ragged flesh and cloth spiked by the broken edges of his ribcage.

'Simon,' wailed Maitland. 'Simon.' He dropped to his knees.

'Leave him.' Talebov was standing over him. 'He's dead.' As he spoke, he kept firing controlled volleys at their attackers who had now moved outside the Abbey. Yuri was covering Zarev's retreat. Maitland shook the blood from his hands, but it would not go away.

'Move, or I'll leave you behind,' warned Talebov.

A woman appeared in the doorway of the aircraft. She waved them on, then raised her gun and started to fire. Maitland had nowhere to go. He stood up. His sanctuary was in the helicopter. Again his decision had been made for him. He took one last glimpse at Simon, then bent low and started running, followed by Talebov, both men being buffeted by the whirling downdraught.

Nike and his gang raced forward, firing from their hips. Suddenly Yuri let out a cry, and crumpled like an empty sack onto his back, blood gushing from a gaping wound in his thigh.

Talebov slung his weapon around his neck, picked up his fallen comrade and hoisted him over his shoulder. Leonid and Zarev by now had reached the relative safety of the chopper. The woman was at the controls again, still waving them on, urging them to run faster.

Maitland picked up Yuri's weapon. Talebov glared at him, weighed down with his burden, unable to prevent Maitland arming himself. The two men stared at each other in understanding, a frozen tableau in the heat of battle, events not of their own choosing making them allies against a common foe.

Maitland cocked the Uzi and opened fire. He made no attempt to shield himself as he sprayed the open space with a lethal burst. He caught Nike in the abdomen as he tried to charge forward in a last desperate rush to the helicopter. Nike was thrown upwards and backwards by the force of the impact, and he somersaulted, head over heels, his lifeless arms beating the air, to land at the feet of his men.

Maitland and Talebov had climbed on board the helicopter before Nike's men had recovered from the shock of their leader's death.

Aldeburgh, England

Julia sat in the armchair by the front door.

'There's all kinds going on. Mrs Templeton said there was shooting. Two gangs of men. With machine guns. And a helicopter.' The receptionist seemed delighted.

Julia nodded her head. She gazed down at their suitcases. She sat forward and inspected one of the labels. *Barcelona*, it said. In her handwriting.

'The place is swarming with police. Mrs Templeton said there's been seven or eight ambulances sent up there. But I think she's exaggerating. There's only two in this area.'

Julia stood up. 'Is the room still available?'

'Beg your pardon.'

'I would like to stay if the room is free.'

'Oh, yes.' The receptionist checked the list. 'You can have it. Has your husband been delayed?'

'Yes,' said Julia. 'I'll wait here till he comes.'